to Tammy Lyn

The Witch Doctor
A
GARDEN OF HEDONE
ROMANCE

By Jean Maxwell

Great to meet you!
Keep in touch
Jean Maxwell.

Dedication

To campfires bright
whose dancing flames
kept warm the night
and sparked this tale
of Witchly delight.

Chapter One

Doctor VaLor mac Haine withdrew his massive cock from between his patient's legs. There seemed to be no satisfying LuSie von Pecht's voracious pussy. They'd been at it for close to an hour, but even his formidable sexual expertise had not yet brought about a climax.

Her eyes rolled open and fixed upon him with a watery gaze, their gold-brown irises brimming wide with need. He knew this look, one that LuSie reserved solely for begging or guilt-mongering, depending on the situation. VaLor would have none of it.

Sprawled on her back, she lay atop a wide divan that served as his examining table. Her legs were spread wide before him, and her breasts spilled over the partly unlaced corset fitted around her torso. Her chest heaved up and down with every breath.

"Your treatment is over," he said, rising from the divan. His tone of voice indicated that LuSie should get dressed and be on her way. Although he cared for her in many ways, these weekly visits had become tiresome and unsatisfying for both of them.

"But Doctor, I am still wanting more," LuSie panted. "How can you leave me like this? I am not yet cured." She licked her plump red lips, sustaining the pleaful stare that VaLor both adored and detested.

"There is no cure for you, LuSie. I think we both know that." He zipped his pants and reached for his white dress shirt as though he'd completed nothing more interesting than his gym workout. "Time's up, you old dear. I have other duties to attend."

Unkempt wisps of her jet-black hair, laced with gray, stuck to her face in sweaty tendrils. "You're a torturer, VaLor," she said, the cherry-red lips rising into a pout.

"No, I'm your doctor," he replied, turning his back on her and striding across the office toward his desk.

LuSie sniffed and rose from the examining table, stuffing her breasts into her corset — a lacy affair detailed with satin bows and tiny bead-pearls along the seams. "I don't understand it, darling. I used to cause earthquakes with my orgasms, you know. Now I can't even tip over a lamp. What's wrong with me?"

"I'm afraid you've finally reached that age, Lu. You're going through the change," he said without looking at her. "It's nothing to be ashamed of, it's quite natural."

LuSie moaned in despair. "Oh, say it isn't so, VaLor. I can't bear the thought of getting old." She leaned over the sink to examine herself in the mirror that hung above. VaLor caught a good look of her buttocks as they protruded toward him in her bent-over stance. He turned away, lessening the chance he might grow hard again. He opened an apothecary cabinet that hung on the wall next to his desk and selected two vials.

He turned to face LuSie as she swung a glittering black cape over her shoulders in dramatic fashion. "Look at the bright side, baby," he said. "If you were mortal, you'd have been old about a hundred years ago. Now take your medicine and find a nice place to rest for a few days. You'll feel good as a young witchling in no time." He handed her the vials.

"I want sex and you give me potions." She hung her head in abject disappointment.

VaLor felt pity for her. With his shirt still unbuttoned, he stepped around his desk and stood close to her. He lifted away a swath of her black hair and kissed the nape of her neck. In a low voice he said, "I can only do so much, sweet. You wear me out." He blew a warm, caressing breath over her pale skin before moving away.

LuSie managed a begrudging smile and turned to leave. VaLor slapped her backside as she did so. In that instant, one of VaLor's paintings fell from its mount on the wall and struck the hardwood floor with a smack. He looked at LuSie and laughed.

"See? You're feeling better already."

She threw him an exasperated look, and without another word, spun on her heel and disappeared through the wall. She did not bother using the door as most witchfolk did to blend in with mortal society. Over the centuries, many things had required adjustment to avoid detection, including the spelling and pronunciation of their names. LuSie became Lucie, VaLor became Valor or sometimes Val. His own surname had been 'mortalized' to McCaine instead of the ancient mac Haine.

Valor's broad shoulders de-tensed in relief after she'd gone. God, he was bored with his job. Bored with his patients, and bored with life in general. As he turned away, he caught his reflection in the mirror over the sink. The familiar face stared back at him. A pair of intense violet eyes, and a mane of flowing dark hair that reached to his shoulders. He considered his image for a moment. His well-muscled chest showed plainly through his open shirt.

He stood six-foot-one and saw not a wrinkle on his clean-shaven face. Not bad for a warlock pushing two hundred, he supposed.

Yet he felt utterly alone. No woman had shared his bed with him in any meaningful way since Artizia had died. Even the lustful Lucie could not stem his loneliness. How many years ago now? He avoided trying to count them, for they made him feel that much closer to death himself. Since then, he'd devoted his time to his patients and to fighting the dreadful pandemic of the Némesati virus.

Artizia had been one of its victims, spurring his determination to isolate the origin of the virus, and ultimately find its cure. Beautiful Artizia, with blue-black hair that fell to her waist, and eyes of fiery amber that drove him to surrender to his basest desires with a single glance. Had there been time, he'd have married her, perhaps even started a family. But fate rendered it not so. Valor chose not to dwell on it, because if he truly gave in to the depths of his grief he'd be lost.

He didn't feel the need to tell Lucie that her symptoms were unmistakably those of the early stages of the Némesati. All over his known world, witchkind had succumbed to some form of the disease that deteriorated their kinetic powers to the point of being no better than mortals, unable to cast the simplest of spells or move the smallest object. Valor feared that the virus also shortened his kinds' inherent longevity. Many witches and warlocks now experienced death as early as one hundred fifty years, well below the average historical lifespan.

He forced the memories away and focused on the present. The one thing that could give meaning to any of it would be finding the cure.

Valor checked his watch. Nearly two p.m. Lucie's appointment had gone overtime and the pharmacy below should have already opened for the afternoon. Damn these needful witches! In delivering their various treatments, sexual and otherwise, they caused him to neglect the lucrative retail business that allowed him to continue his research. If he would ever break the code of the Némesati, it would be with the aid of modern science combined with his own powers of 'craft.

He went to the mirror once more, buttoned the front of his crisp white shirt, and groomed his hair and fingernails before taking the back stairs down to his shop.

*

Darcy deHavalend jumped onto the curb, narrowly missing a speeding bike messenger.

"Holy shit," she swore, pulling her earbuds out and staring after the crazy cyclist. She'd been so lost in her music she'd absentmindedly stepped onto the road, and hadn't seen him coming until the last second.

Geez, wake up girlfriend, she scolded herself. *Gonna get yourself killed before the end of the semester if you don't watch out.* Making the trek from the University of Massachusetts campus to her tiny studio apartment took nearly an hour each way, and she adjusted her weighty backpack to take the strain off her shoulders for the remainder of the journey.

Today's lecture offered no help at all. Darcy couldn't wait to get home and delve into more promising research than the windbag Professor Harkin had to impart. For a man so accomplished in microbiology, Harkin had no concept of how to apply his knowledge to greater discoveries in viral dissemination.

Something Harkin said today did spark an idea, though. He'd talked about a "chain reaction" of bacteria, induced by certain control conditions that just might be the breakthrough

Darcy sought. However, even if her formula worked she couldn't tell anyone about it. She just hoped to develop an effective serum before time ran out. She had to. The lives of her mother and grandmother hung in the balance.

The warm autumn day made her wipe the sweat from her forehead. As she crossed the intersection at Cambridge Street, she saw a familiar sign overhead. McCaine's Pharmacy. She'd passed it every day since she'd moved to Boston, always meaning to go in, but never seeming to find the nerve.

The small shop seemed out of place, sandwiched between two modern high-tech stores. Its quaint exterior looked quite unlike the mega-drugmarts scattered throughout Boston. McCaine's Pharmacy exuded a charm – for lack of a better word – that the others did not. While curious, she was skeptical as to the type and quality of the merchandise within. She might be wasting her time looking there. But the materials she needed for her test formulas were hard to find, and something told her they might be inside McCaine's.

Darcy stopped beneath the awning that shaded the entrance. Were they closed? The place seemed dark inside. As if in answer to her unspoken question, an electronic switch buzzed at the door, and a neon sign flickered to life in the window.

OPEN.

She stepped back a pace, amused by the shop's timely awakening. Inhaling a long breath and arching an eyebrow, she pushed open the door and marched in.

The interior seemed as rustic as the storefront outside. Wide wooden floor planks creaked beneath her DC skate shoes. Tall shelves, overloaded with jars and bottles, lined the walls. Stepping closer, she felt a slight wave of disappointment as she read their labels. Ordinary brand names found in a thousand other pharmacies across the country.

She browsed the remaining shelves, hoping for something a little more exotic. The shop's lighting left a little to be desired, but the scent inside certainly enticed. Fresh, yet sharp. Not clinical at all. It reminded Darcy of cracked peppercorns, and she wondered if there might be a perfume counter. As she circled the room, her wish for something exotic came true.

Her breath caught as she glimpsed a dark-haired man standing at the back of the shop. His wavy hair fell nearly to his shoulders and his chiselled features were bronzed to perfection. He'd just begun to pull on a lab coat when he spotted her.

"Good afternoon," he said, stopping his arm in mid-sleeve. He smiled, then shrugged the coat into place over his broad shoulders. "Can I help you, young lady?"

Darcy's feet seemed frozen to the floor. His gaze alone made her legs turn to rubber. *Young lady?* Yes, she supposed that to this mature man she must look an adolescent fright, dressed in shorts and skateboard shoes and her reddish-gold mane of hair tamed beneath a cheap plastic headband. If she had to guess, she'd peg him for at least thirty-five, but who cared? When he looked at her with those eyes that glittered like amethysts, his age was the last thing on her mind.

Speak, her subconscious screamed. Darcy's mouth opened, only to utter an idiotic, "umm." The man stepped closer. She swore electricity emanated from him by the way her hair stood on end as he approached.

"Yes," she said, recovering her voice. "I'm looking for some herbal compounds." Her feet still would not move. She watched him lean against the counter, regarding her intensely. Jesus, that violet stare could melt a chocolate bar from across the room.

"Herbal compounds," he repeated. "Such as?"

Darcy's confidence wavered. *His tone is already making me feel foolish. I've made a mistake coming in here.* But since she stood rooted to the spot, she cleared her throat and pressed on. "Yarrow, Bittersweet, Witch Hazel," she said. "I mean, *Achillea millefolium, Solanum dulcamara*, and…" She blushed at the realization she could not remember the latin term for Witch Hazel. Her eyes went wide in embarrassment. "Witch Hazel," she repeated, resorting to its common name.

The man raised himself to his full height, his public smile switching to an amused grin. "I see. Tablets, or gelcaps?"

Darcy's blush flowed through her entire face. She could hide nothing now. Despite its outward appearance, this place was as any other modern drugstore, offering nothing but pills and cough syrup. Agh, she wished she'd never opened her mouth. But in for a penny, in for a pound. "Uh, no. I'd rather hoped for some dried organics, or essential oils."

His unusual eyes seemed to darken in amusement. "Did you, now? Not much call for that type of thing. But let's see what we have."

She shuffled nervously from side to side while she watched him hunt down her ingredients. Damn, she hadn't even thought about how much these might cost. She hoped she had enough money to cover it. On a student's budget, cash wasn't readily found in Darcy's wallet.

After several minutes he returned from the back shelves with a small paper envelope and a plastic vial. He smiled at Darcy once more, as though in apology. Darcy took a deep breath. Any kind of smile from this man seemed worth more than gold. She found herself thinking of the next occasion she might have to visit McCaine's Pharmacy.

"I'm sorry, young lady. But two out of three isn't bad." He held up the little envelope. "Dried yarrow." He set it down, then lifted the vial. "Witch hazel extract. Both reasonably common." He slid them together across the polished counter toward her. "But the other, no luck. Bittersweet has several varieties, all of them poisonous. I'm afraid you won't find them in a refined form."

"Oh." She felt speechless under his affecting grin. What else could she say? If he didn't have it, he didn't have it. Her formula might not work without all three components. She'd have to get it some other way. But where? She swallowed, her throat dry.

"Do you know which strain you're looking for?" he asked, seeming to sense her disappointment. "If you can wait a few days, I might be able to get some of the common plant." He pulled a business card from a holder at the edge of the counter and flipped it to her between his first and second fingers. Darcy reached out to take the card, letting her own fingers touch his. Oh, what she wouldn't do to have those graceful things caressing other parts of her body.

Darcy Merinda deHavalend! She could practically hear her mother's voice in her head. Such naughty thoughts! "That's very kind of you," she said, certain that her face must be aflame with color by now. "When should I come back?"

His dark-haired head tilted slightly to one side. "Call the number on Friday. I should know by then." His glance fell over her as if sizing her up to fit a coffin. "Good day, Miss…?" His open-ended sentence seemed to ask for both her name and her exit at the same time.

"Darcy," she said. "Thank you, I'll…uh…call Friday." She backed away toward the door, holding up the card in gesture.

His brow furrowed. "Don't forget your herbal compounds."

She stopped in mid-step, having the distinct sensation of the shop shrinking around her. She felt dizzy from the heat rising off her chest. She must look like an idiot. She certainly felt like one. "Oh. Yes." She managed a crooked smile. "How much?"

He picked up the items and walked around the counter to meet her. "I'll put in on account. We'll settle up when you come next." He handed her the containers. "Fair enough, Miss Darcy?"

"Thank you," she said, her voice a breathy whisper. With her embarrassment leaping off the scale, she turned and ran out of the shop.

Chapter Two

At the end of the block, Darcy slowed her pace and leaned against the trunk of one of the giant Ash trees that lined the street. She took a close look at the business card she clutched in one hand, the packaged ingredients still cradled in the other.

Dr. V. McCaine, MD, MSc Pharm, Owner.

A doctor! Not just a pharmacist. And a Masters' degree too. Holy cow. *Congratulations on making a horse's ass of yourself in front of the most educated person in the city,* she mocked herself. Miss Darcy? Egad, she couldn't even get her own name right in his presence. She lowered herself onto a park bench next to the tree.

"Way too old for me," she murmured aloud. A man like that couldn't possibly be interested in a college student like herself. What even gave her that idea? Ridiculous. Under the shade of the Ash branches, she took a closer look at the goods she held in her hands. She hadn't even specified the quantities; Dr. McCaine seemed to know exactly how much to dispense. About an ounce of the dried yarrow lay in the envelope, and twenty-five mils of witch hazel in the vial. A decent sized batch of serum could be produced, even with these small amounts.

Tucking the containers into her backpack, she hesitated with the business card. She closed her eyes and smelled it, swiping the few inches of its length beneath her nostrils. The scent uploaded to her olfactory database. Dr. McCaine now had a permanent record stored in Darcy's brain. A record that not only included his cologne, but his *kathra*, his sensual identity.

She opened her eyes and glanced about, hastily slipping the card into the same compartment of her pack. She felt a tiny bit ashamed of this strange talent. For as long as she could remember, objects, clothing, or even strands of hair, could all carry a signature scent that Darcy could receive, record and recall at any time. It became her personal chemistry catalogue for identifying people and things just as uniquely as their DNA. It just looked a little weird, sometimes, her sniffing about like a tracking dog. On the upside, it served her academic scores well.

Another twenty-minute walk saw her entering her small apartment on Beacon Street. Darcy's makeshift chemistry lab waited inside, claiming most of her limited counter space and overtaking a good portion of the bathroom, too. Oliviah dashed into the hallway as soon as Darcy opened her door. The agile calico feline did not take kindly to being locked in all day, and never failed to make the touchdown rush whenever she had the chance.

"Oliviah," Darcy called, "get back in here. Now's not the time, you silly cat!"

"Yeah, yeah, wait until nightfall, I know. Always the night. Can't you think of something better to call me than 'cat'?"

Oliviah's words sounded only within Darcy's head. Along with her arcane olfactory skill, the fact that she could commune with her pet cat also ranked high among her family secrets.

"I'll call you worse than that, missy. Get inside, now!"

Oliviah leaped down from the staircase newel post she'd perched on at the end of the hall, and landed lightly on all fours. *"Oh, I'm terrified! Just don't call me late for dinner."* The cat sauntered into the apartment, head and tail held high.

Darcy closed the door, dead-bolting it for good measure. The landlord didn't know about Oliviah, and she planned to keep it that way. She'd let her out the window when night fell, allowing her to blend into the dark with the rest of the city-kitty population for her exercise and entertainment.

"Look what I got today," Darcy said, unloading her backpack. "The missing ingredients. Some of them, anyway." She took the herbal compounds over to her kitchen lab and began to measure out an experimental amount of each into crucibles.

Oliviah yawned and washed her face with one paw. *"Spare me the boring details. The only ingredient I'm interested in is Friskies. When's chow time?"*

"You wouldn't be so hungry if your life was at stake. Think about Mom and Grandma, will you? If this works, you'll be up to your whiskers in food with all three of us feeding you. Have some compassion, or at least some willpower."

With that, Oliviah stalked away to a plastic storage tote that served as her kitty bed and curled up inside it.

Darcy ignored her and continued with her preparations. A shame about the Bittersweet. She felt certain it held a crucial element to the bacterial chain reaction she hoped to produce, and time was running out. Over many months, she'd watched her mother and grandmother's symptoms worsen. Her mom had aged far in advance of her years, enough that the pair looked more like sisters than mother and daughter.

Her grandma's arthritis and osteoporosis had increased at an alarming rate, virtually crippling her overnight. The virus, or whatever it was, had both accelerated their illnesses, and stripped them of their natural talents.

Their ability to mindspeak with her, similar to the way that she and Oliviah communicated, had vanished completely. Those ultra-private conversations had guided and comforted Darcy all her life, and she missed them terribly.

In addition, their psychokinetic skills were failing. The ability to travel and to visit friends around the world in an overnight, or transform their indoor and garden spaces into idyllic paradises that changed daily, had kept the light in her mom and grandma's eyes, and happiness in their hearts. But now, this sickness had taken it all away from them.

Darcy always knew that her family wielded preternatural powers, though she herself had only the mindspeak and sensory tools. She'd never questioned it until she made the decision to enter University and had to confront a basic fact:

The deHavalends were not normal.

Her degree in Chemistry would be complete in another two years. She hoped her mom would hold out at least that long, and with any luck perhaps she'd find the cure even sooner. To gain access to brilliant minds, state-of-the-art facilities and centuries of historical data, she'd left her mom and grandma behind in Phoenix to enroll at the University of Massachusetts. Sadly, Professor Harkin didn't fall into the brilliant minds category in her opinion, but the campus offered scores of other resource people.

After today's visit to McCaine's Pharmacy, she realized that school wasn't the only place to find brilliance. Dr. McCaine certainly appeared to have smarts, judging by his business card. As she ground the bits of dried yarrow into a juicy mush with mortar and pestle, the doctor's handsome face formed in her mind's eye. She recalled his *kathra*, as well. Dark undertones of rich musk, a middle layer of forest, topped with wildberry highlights melded in a potent melange of mystery and masculinity. Something else entwined itself in the recipe, too…a scintillating thread of, of….what? Darcy struggled to identify the substance. Not an aroma so much as a structure, a spinal cord of will, of pure being.

The more she focused on it, the more she sensed her body growing lethargic, sleepy yet not ready for sleep. She exhaled with force, to clear the *kathra* from her consciousness. She needed to be alert to continue her experiment. She now felt certain there was more to the gorgeous doctor than appeared on the surface; and the surface looked pretty damn fine to begin with. Just the simple touch of his fingers over the counter had sent her glands into hyperdrive. If she hoped to work with him on a scientific level, she'd be hard pressed to retain her objectivity.

Darcy! She scolded herself. She hadn't much experience with men, and the good doctor would be a terrible place to start an education in that area. Besides, he'd given no hint of interest in return; just doing his job. Throwing herself at him wouldn't serve anyone's purpose, as much as her hormones clamored for her to do so. His value lay in his knowledge; that much she must remember.

"My, my. Someone's gotten under your skin, haven't they?" From her coiled position in the shallow totebox, Oliviah's tail undulated back and forth while her golden eyes fixed Darcy with an all-knowing gaze.

"Shut up, you." *Damn that cat all to hell.* Oliviah's communication did not limit itself to Darcy's spoken voice. On occasion, the animal could read her thoughts as well, particularly when they involved her more carnal instincts. She often forgot Oliviah's age. Each of her nine lives could easily span 50 years, and the cat had belonged to both her grandmother and mother before residing with Darcy. No point disregarding her vast experience.

Returning to her experiment, she strained the yarrow essence into two petrie dishes, then added a drop of witch hazel to each. She recorded the date, conditions and amounts on her computer tablet. A tabletop refrigerator occupied considerable space on her kitchen counter, and from it Darcy drew a test tube rack of blood samples. Selecting one tube, she extracted a few mils with a syringe, and placed three dots into the petrie dish mixture. She repeated the process with a second dish, and a second blood sample from another tube.

Nothing to do now but wait. She returned the tubes to the refrigerator, covered the dishes and placed them in the test environment; in this case, a Styrofoam cooler with low-wattage task lamps clamped to the sides. The finest equipment a student budget could buy.

*

Valor locked the pharmacy doors and switched off the lights. His afternoon had passed without much incident, just the usual customers picking up prescriptions and a few youngsters in search of their favorite candy bars. The youth's presence had reminded him of his earlier visitor, the girl named Darcy. He'd lived in Boston a long time, and had never seen her before, with her bouncy strawberry-blond curls and fresh, freckled face.

Despite the ingenuous exterior, something about her bespoke of an innate wisdom, Her posterior, he'd noticed, wasn't bad either. But much too young to be of serious interest, barely out of the womb compared to himself. She looked no more than twenty or so, and he with nearly two centuries under his belt had no right to admire her juicy buns, nice as they were.

He suspected she was a good student, too. What sort of studies did she undertake, he wondered, seeking out plant extracts and essential oils? The varieties she asked for piqued his curiosity. He hadn't thought about the healing qualities of yarrow root, its properties known for stimulating cognitive thought. It might pertain to the cerebral short-circuiting so evident in many of the Némesati cases he'd documented. Perhaps Miss Darcy was on to something, whether she knew it or not. He made a mental note to review all three of the herbs she'd requested, and decide if they had any synergistic effect when used together.

As Valor hung his labcoat and prepared to climb upstairs, the back door rattled with the impact of frantic fists pounding upon it. The sun had set, and the light outside illuminated a figure huddling underneath it. Her wild eyes were dilated, whether with drugs or fear he couldn't tell, and he hurried to let her enter.

The woman fell across the threshold as Valor opened the door. He caught her on the way down, her blond hair falling in masses across her face and shoulders.

"Shania," he said. "What's happened? What are you doing here?"

Chapter Three

"VaLor," Shania gasped, sinking to her knees in his embrace. "Help me."

Valor eased her to the floor, crouching next to her and holding her face to the light with one hand under her chin. He knew this witch — the daughter of his best friend, JuLyan, who had also been a victim of the Némesati. ShaNia, as was her traditional name, disappeared after her father JuLyan's death some years ago. Even as a young witchling she'd been pretty. Now Valor saw that a few years had added to her beauty. But at the moment, her fair face showed red blotches, dotted with specks of dirt and vomit. Her white-blond hair flew unkempt in bristled thatches about her shoulders, reaching nearly to the floor in its overgrown length.

"Shania," he said again. "Are you injured? Speak to me."

Her breath came in heaving pants, and her eyes focused on him as he held her face in the V between his thumb and fingers. "I…I'm so c-cold," she whimpered. "I'm sick… look…look at my face." Tears welled up and spilled down one cheek, then the other. "My face," she said again before collapsing into sobs.

Close up, Valor could see the scattered blotches in varying shades of red covering her pretty face in random patches, some larger, some smaller. The larger ones had open centers, threatening to ooze blood and other fluids any second. "It's alright," he soothed. "We'll take care of it, come inside now. You're safe here."

He raised her up as he stood. With her crying and blubbering showing no signs of stopping, he swooped one arm beneath her buttocks and lifted her into his arms. She didn't weigh much, but Valor, as with all warlocks, had the strength to carry several full grown humans if he chose to. He carried her upstairs to his home above the pharmacy.

The upper floor housed not only his office and examining area, but two bedrooms, a lounge and galley-style kitchen. He laid Shania in the guest bedroom and removed her crumpled cape from around her body. With a wave of his index finger, a bowl of warm liquid and several clean gauze cloths appeared on the nightstand. He laid her head on the pillow and leaned over to bathe her tortured face with the steaming mixture from the bowl.

"There now, tell me what's happened. You're going to be fine, I'll see to that."

"Thank you," Shania said, her crying reduced to sorrowful sniffs. "I didn't know where else to go. He'll be coming after me, I know it."

"Who?" Valor's treatment had stemmed the redness and swelling in her face, and she looked much more like her pretty self again. He'd not seen the virus cause this kind of symptom before. He hoped these lesions were of some other mortal disease. One he could deal with, not some mutation of an already virulent affliction he had no answer for.

Shania's dark eyes turned luminous as she tried to speak. Her lips didn't seem to want to form the next words. "Germayne," she said, finally.

Valor's heart went stiff. Even the sound of his former colleague's name still stung him to the core. His brother in arms. His benefactor. His enemy. He had returned then, from his self-imposed exile. "Germayne. Why would he be after you," he asked, after a long silence.

Shania's expression turned miserable once more. "I'm so ashamed. I…we…lived together. For awhile. After father's death, I ran away. I didn't know what I was doing. I lived crazy, I took drugs; fell in with the wrong sort. I don't remember when he found me, exactly. Only that he saved me from certain death, and brought me back here, to Boston." She closed her eyes, squeezing back tears that were building again.

"Lived together," Valor repeated, his guts starting to turn. "As what? Roommates? Business partners? What?" He had a feeling he wouldn't like her answer.

She rolled her head back and forth in denial. "No. I had no choice. We lived as lovers."

This knowledge, though anticipated, sunk like a stone in to the pit of Valor's stomach. The lecherous and arrogant old fart. Taking advantage of the innocent in the most painful way possible. How far he'd strayed from the ideals they once held together. And how typical.

"I'd rather have died," she said, "If I'd known what he'd make me do…what he would do to me. I should have died on the street in peace."

"Now, now, I won't hear that kind of talk," Valor interrupted. "You're here with me. No matter what he's done, or will do, you're safe with me, do you understand?" He arranged the long locks of near-white hair over her shoulders and chest, smoothing them into place. He smiled at her, to divert her attention from the gravity of her situation. "Say yes."

With a little urging, Shania's lovely lips formed a feeble

smile. "Yes, Valor." Her hand reached up and covered his as it lay curled around a swath of her hair.

"Alright then. Rest. Are you hungry? Thirsty?"

Shania looked into his eyes, saying nothing. She moved his hand down her chest so that his palm settled over her breast. Valor pretended not to notice, but with that gesture he couldn't help but glance at the rest of her. Underneath her cape she'd worn a white satin shirt, almost like a man's shirt, with several top buttons undone and the soft mounds of her breasts partially revealed. The shirttails barely reached to her hips and fell open in the center, showing the triangle of pink panties that covered her pussy. She nudged her thighs apart a little as his gaze lingered there.

Enough. He lifted his hand away and straightened. "I'll bring you some water."

Valor left the room to fetch a glass for her. Shania's surprise visit brought more complications than he'd bargained for. The return of GerMayne, an extremely powerful warlock, shot dread into his heart like a bullet. That in itself meant bad news, but the suffering he'd brought to a naive young witch was quite unforgivable. Topping it off, Shania's experiences had clearly left her with inappropriate values, making her stay here an awkward and difficult one. He hoped her father, his dear departed friend Julyan, would forgive him if circumstances got out of control.

*

Lucie sat at her favorite coffee shop with mug in hand and dark glasses covering her eyes as she gazed out into the street. Her visit to the doctor yesterday hadn't gone as well as she'd hoped. Having sex with VaLor mac Haine had become a ritual; one she enjoyed immensely. The warlock's magnificent cock and magic hands did wonders for her ego and her condition. She'd known him for most of their considerable lives, and though she wished otherwise, still had a crush on him.

Lately though, even his venerable skills in lovemaking hadn't been enough to make her feel well, feel like her old self again. Orgasm after orgasm still hadn't moved any mountains, and even achieving climax had become more difficult and time consuming for her. Poor dear Valor. Perhaps he spoke the truth when he said she'd worn him out. She just couldn't get enough sex. Even though he accommodated her on a regular basis, she knew deep down he would never love her. Not the way he'd loved Artizia.

That old wound still ached. Artizia…the golden eyed girl. Who could compete with that? Honor student, captain of the airborne cheer squad, artist and poet. Everyone loved her, even Lucie in her own way. She attracted loyalty and admiration, without even trying. And best of all, she'd attracted Valor. They'd made a star couple, no one could argue that.

But it all came to an end when Artizia died. Lucie's pangs of jealousy still intermingled with sadness at the loss of the beautiful witch ArtiZia le Manze. Strange, her illness had come on so rapidly…no one really knew the cause of it. One by one, her powers had gone out, extinguished like sputtering candles, and her skin clouded with premature age. Lucie recalled all this with renewed intensity, a nagging voice in her mind whispering that the same might be her fate. Her puzzling symptoms that resisted treatment could just be variations on a theme of whatever mysterious malady had claimed Artizia.

Lucie's coffee mug shattered in her hand, her grip and her thoughts so intense it crushed the ceramic to bits, sending the creamy contents splattering in all directions. A few patrons turned to gawk, and without missing a beat, Lucie passed a dripping hand over the broken shards, the pieces reassembling and hot coffee refilling itself. A second gesture with her pinky finger carved an arc in the direction of the questioning faces. They all went back to their drinks and pastries without comment.

At least some of her basic skills were still intact. This gave Lucie some comfort as she sipped her rematerialized brew, returning to her view of the busy street in front of her. A bus traveled northbound, and as it passed from sight, Lucie nearly broke her cup a second time with what she saw next.

He stood there at the stop, as if he'd just fallen off the moving bus. But this man needed no buses, taxis or aircraft to deliver him wherever he wanted to go. He spotted her immediately, as though he'd been expecting her there, and started across the street toward her. Lucie sat up straight, waiting for his arrival but not signaling him in any way. It wasn't necessary. His long dress coat flapped roguishly in the wind as he stepped onto the curb and took a seat at her table.

"Hello, LuSie. Been a long time." His jet-black hair with its streaks of white, much like her own, glistened in the morning light. She didn't think him handsome exactly; striking, yes. But then, all warlocks had stunning features of one kind or another.

"Hello GerMayne," she responded, mirroring his pronunciation of her traditional name.

GerMayne au Coin, the most formidable and despised warlock on the continent, studied her up and down. "You're looking…well. Surprised to see me?" He raised an index finger, and a tall café latte appeared in midair in front of him, at exactly the right height for his finger to wrap around its handle and lift the cup to his lips.

"Quite. What brings you here?"

"Let's say I got homesick," he replied, a one-sided grin revealing pearly, pointed teeth.

Lucie laughed. He'd always been a strange one, with a sense of humour to match. "That's a good one. Got any more jokes for me today?"

Germayne set his mug aside. "Do you know what you get when you cross a witch with a doctor?"

Lucie's laughter faded. "No. What?"

"A dead doctor."

Her face went rigid. "I don't get it."

"You will," he replied, his expression lightening. He waved his palm over the table, and a rectangular box materialized, one Lucie recognized. "How about a game? We had some great matches at this, you and me."

The hinged box split open, revealing a game board and playing pieces. Dragonchess. Lucie's smile returned. She loved a good old game of Dragonchess, particularly when she could beat an old consort at the pursuit.

"High dice goes first?" She reached for the dice barrel and gave it a shake.

"Of course," he nodded.

Lucie's dice tumbled out of the barrel landing at twelve. "Ha. I win already." She chose her playing piece, the Chalice, and plopped it on the starting square. Germayne chose the Horse Head, and gestured for her to roll again.

A seven this time, Lucie moved her marker onto square seven, advancing diagonally across the board rather than in linear sequence. Player's choice. Germayne scooped the dice, rolled a ten and skipped ahead of her on the same path. Each square on the board held a symbol with specific meaning, much like a Tarot deck. Lucie had the option of rolling again, but called "stay." Her opponent rolled a second time, scoring a four. He moved the appropriate squares and set the dice aside. He looked at Lucie, indicating with a raised eyebrow that she should interpret.

She looked at her square, the Enchantress, and cocked

her head to one side, garnering its meaning in this instance. "There's trouble with a woman. A witch, not mortal. She will be either a help or a hindrance." She leaned back in her chair, indicating Germayne's turn.

His token had landed on the Stablemaster. A safe bet. Typically not worldshaking, but one never knew what happened where Germayne was concerned. He stared at the board for a moment, rubbing his fingertips together as he deciphered his move.

"The world is out of control. One master will emerge, and all others pledge allegiance or die." He looked directly at Lucie. "Which would you prefer?"

Lucie snickered, then realized Germayne wasn't truly playing Dragonchess with her. He favored a different game entirely. The object of Dragonchess involved fortune telling, but intended as frivolity, not true prophecy. "Between service or death? That's a no-brainer…why would you ask such a question?'

"Because, my dear little cousin, you, and every one of our kind, will be making that choice. Soon." His purplish lips peeled back in a smile that revealed the full range of his toothy countenance. "Your move."

Lucie's hand reached for the dice barrel, but kept her eyes on her foe. Cousin indeed, but enemy just the same. Not to be trusted nor allied with, blood relative or no. She rolled another seven, a good omen, but her Chalice landed on the Woodsman. She pursed her lips while considering her interpretation.

"The master has an obstacle. A brave hunter will cross his path, do not underestimate him." Lucie returned Germayne's horrid stare. "Or her."

The slightest trace of surprise jerked at the corner of Germayne's mouth. Ha. She'd caught him with that one. He didn't expect a female adversary. She had no idea if that would prove to be true, but wanted to confound him at all costs. Undermining his confidence had often worked on him in the past, when they were younger. If anyone knew Germayne's strengths and weaknesses, Lucie did.

"Your turn," she said with an equally threatening grin. "Or would you like to quit now?"

"Not until we determine a winner. It's yet to be decided". This time he levitated the shaker barrel and the dice leapt into it of their own accord. He rotated his index finger in the air a few times and the barrel spun around before spilling its contents onto the board.

Snake Eyes.

He moved his marker two spaces ahead without touching them. The Horse Head jiggled into position on the Faerie square. This interpretation Lucie couldn't wait to hear. Faeries never foretold anything important, and what little they did reveal wasn't to be believed. She chuckled under her breath, anticipating her triumph.

"The faeries have retreated underground. They know what shakes the earth, and they know when to hide. The scourge is upon us, and only the clever will survive."

Germayne's rhyming words echoed so forcefully that Lucie's jaw dropped just a little. He couldn't be serious. Just a mind game, she reasoned. *To get me onside with whatever mischief he's planning. To hell with that.* She scooped up the playing tokens from the board.

"Germayne. I think this game is void. You're not following the rules."

Germayne waved his hand, closing up the board and sending it back from whence it came. He reached for his coffee and took a long sip, licking his lips in exaggerated enjoyment. When he looked at her again, he spoke. "You're right. I'm not following the rules. I'm making them."

Chapter Four

Darcy awoke to a pair of amber eyes staring her down. She jerked her head away, and bucked the insolent animal off her chest. Oliviah spilled off the edge of the bed, landing predictably on her feet in cat fashion.

"Yowl. Good Morning to you, too, Goldilocks."

"Get off me, you little skank. What's the big idea? I'm tired…I don't have class until noon. Lemme sleep in, will you?" Darcy rolled over, yanking her comforter over her head. The light pressure of four paws landed stubbornly on top of her again.

"Oh, I think you'll want to get up, sunshine. Your experiment needs a little attention."

Darcy's eyes shot open as she threw back the comforter. "What? What would you know about my experiment? You said it bored you to death."

Oliviah leapt off the bed and trotted toward the kitchen. *"You bore me to death. Not your experiments."*

Darcy rolled out of bed, tugging down her tee shirt that served as a nightgown, and followed Oliviah. The Styrofoam incubator jiggled and tossed as if something boiled inside it.

She ran to it, grabbing hold and steadying it before it could rattle right off the countertop. The sides felt warm, and she pulled the plug on the clamp lights.

Peering over the edge, her two petrie dishes bubbled and fizzed, their contents swelling up and then collapsing like fried eggs gone bad. Both mixtures glowed shades of red and orange, the pulsing bubbles making an evil hissing noise. Finally, one burst completely, firing a slimy glob straight up to stick to the ceiling like a primordial spitball.

The pair stared at the miscreant substance, and the pendulous drip that threatened to fall from it.

"Holy shit," Darcy whispered. "What in blazes would cause that?

Oliviah swished her tail in thought. *"I think it's your missing ingredients. You sure you bought the right stuff?"*

"Yes, yes, I'm sure," Darcy muttered, fitting on a pair of rubber gloves to remove the petrie dishes from the incubator. A thought occurred to her. Actually, I didn't buy it. I still owe the man. Now it doesn't even work. Shit. Well, I'll give him what for on Friday."

"How do you know it didn't work? Aren't you going to analyze your samples?"

The red-orange goo began to harden inside the containers. Darcy realized she would have to smear the slides right away in order to create readable cross-sections. "Yeah, I'm gonna analyze them. I wish I had my own scope; it'll have to wait until I get to campus."

"Maybe Dr. Wonderful has a...tool...you can borrow." Oliviah said, winking a golden eye.

Darcy shot her a slanted look. "Mind your own business." She readied the smears with what remained of the sample mixtures and slid them into the tiny refrigerator. Not a bad idea. She would have to see Dr. McCaine one way or another. He might have some valuable insight on the results.

As for "tools," she didn't need Oliviah's help in imagining the doctor's equipment. She'd done enough of that already.

She made the trek to the University ahead of schedule, to grab a spot in the lab before class started. The imaging of her samples displayed a panoply of cellular confusion. Patterns that resembled nothing she'd ever seen before. With a sigh, she began making what sense she could, increasing the magnification in the hopes of finding something familiar.

The red blood cells on the first sample were her mother's, and the second, her grandmother's. Each one showed different results, which made no sense at all. The damaged cells from her mom appeared to have multiplied with the application of her new serum; bummer. But her grandmother's sample showed neither an increase or decrease in the number of infected cells. Worse, it showed what appeared to be an entirely new kind of cell, some extraneous by-product of the chemical reaction. Darcy could not determine if they were inert or malignant. Either way, her scientific subconscious felt troubled by this. She might be in way over her head on this one, with no authority she felt safe in consulting.

Except maybe one.

*

Shania's sleeping form seemed like paradise personified. Valor stood at the edge of her bed, looking her over for any sign of distress. Her breathing even and her countenance peaceful, she didn't appear to be sick in any way. All too well, Valor knew the symptoms of the virus to be unpredictable and wide-ranging. From nothing at all to Lucie's sexual addictions to the disgusting lesions which had astonishingly disappeared from Shania's face since last night. He knew his treatment had helped, but not enough to justify her now pristinely clear complexion.

He had to leave soon. He'd made an appointment with an herbology expert at the Faculty of Pharmacy this morning, to research the interactions of Darcy's herbal combinations. Shania's revelation about her relationship with Germayne continued to disturb him, as their parting had not been pretty. His last meeting with Germayne had seen the two of them at battlegrips with sharp surgical instruments, each of them prepared to slit the other's throat over principle.

"Let them die," Germayne growled. "The weak must perish. It's the way of things, Valor. Don't try to change it… only the strong should survive."

"If it were your beloved dying, you would not think so." Valor had spat back. "Artizia is my life, how can you not help her? You have the power…use it, for the love of witchkind!"

"If I help her, I would be expected to help them all! There's not enough of me to go around, brother. Remember our old Némesati Jeshua, and the Lepers…it was not his place to save them all, either. You think I am better than Him? You chose to be the doctor, not me. Tend to the sick if you will…see how far it gets you!"

At that, Valor had lunged at his contemporary, scalpel in hand, aiming for his carotid artery. But in cowardly style, Germayne disapparated, unwilling to fight a mortal fight for his convictions. Valor fell to the ground, and knew from that moment forward, he would have to combat the evil of the Némesati alone.

Shania moaned and shifted beneath the covers he'd laid over her the night before. Her legs writhed and her head thrashed from side to side. "No, no…" Her voice rose in fear, escalating into anguished cries. Valor reached for her, holding her head still. Fever radiated from her brow.

"Shania, wake up, it's all right."

She struggled against him for a moment, then opened

her eyes. Her breath came in short, rapid bursts. She relaxed under his touch and her gaze softened into watery solace. "I was dreaming," she whispered.

"I know. But it's over now. Only a dream."

She smiled and wiggled a weak nod. "You were in it," she said.

"Was I, now?" he replied, placing two fingers on her throat to check her pulse. He could feel her body overheating beneath the blankets. She reached up and cast them off the edge of the bed.

"Yes."

At some point during the night she'd removed her shirt and underclothing. Valor took in the sight of her perfect, naked body lying tantalizingly within reach. A crystal stud piercing graced her navel. Her tiny brown nipples formed peaks with the sudden cool of the surrounding air. Her fresh young pussy shone hairless, whether depilated by chemicals or witchcraft he did not know, or care. His cock went rigid.

"You were fighting for me...to get me away from him. So you could take me." She grasped his hand still held at her throat, and lowered it to rest between her legs. His fingers felt the smooth skin of her labia. "Take me now. For real."

"Shania," he admonished. "No. I can't do that. I'm old enough to be your father. Think what he would say if he saw us now, rest his *kathra*. You're my patient. That would be wrong." He pulled his hand away but she held his wrist fast, keeping him in contact with her moist flesh.

"Father is dead. We're alive. I've been so near death I can't remember how it feels. Make me feel alive...please," she said, her voice near begging.

Valor's willpower began to break down. He shouldn't. Wasn't right. No time. If the Némesati infection wracked Shania's young body, would his sexual ministrations help her, as it helped his other patients, like Lucie? His own body's cravings didn't require justification, but his rational mind did. He made a compromise. He reached his healing fingers between her folds to find her clitoris.

Shania drew in a sharp breath. "Yes, oh yes."

He massaged her clit with gentle rotations, increasing pressure in increments. Her cream flowed freely, covering his fingers, allowing him to stroke the full length of her genitals from anus to cleft, back and forth, pausing on her clit for a half-second of each pass. Her hips began to buck, leaning into his touch. Her hands still gripped his wrist, following every motion.

"Does that feel good?" he asked, intending to increase her orgasmic response with verbal stimulation. "You like that, little lady? I'll bet you do, don't you…you're Daddy's bad girl, aren't you?

"Yes, I'm your bad girl, don't stop…" she whispered.

"Such a bad girl," he continued, slipping his middle finger into her vagina and pumping it in and out. "Pretty little pussy, so tight." He added his index finger and pumped her with both. "Tight little girl, come for me. Let yourself come." His fingers withdrew and paddled her swollen clitoris, swathed in her own juices, side to side, increasing his rhythm.

Shania's voice rose into desperate cries. "Yes, do me, give me more. Fuck me, please."

"Let it go, baby, let it go," he encouraged, plunging his thumb into her this time, in and out, in and out. "Sweet little pussy, come for me little one," As Shania dissolved in to incoherent grunts of pleasure, Valor leaned down and sucked on her quivering clit, sending her into convulsions of sexual ecstasy. The force of her reaction manifested itself as a thunderclap outside, in broad daylight. He pressed his tongue against her tender tissues until her screaming and tremors subsided, the thunder reduced to a faraway rumble, and her body quieted in satisfaction. A good sign, the thunder. She wasn't too far gone.

"Oh," she gasped, between gulps of air. Oh, Valor, yes, yes, thank you. You are the greatest…you…I love you. I love you so much."

Valor closed his eyes. He couldn't bear to hear those words. She didn't mean them…couldn't mean them. They were strangers to each other, and he had no purpose other than to ease her symptoms. She didn't know what she said, poor troubled thing. He mourned for her dead father Julyan, mentally begging his forgiveness.

He straightened, rubbing her thighs comfortingly before covering her with the fallen bedclothes. "Rest now," he said, his voice rough with emotion. He left the room unable to speak another word nor entertain another wretched thought. He felt himself drifting further from a solution to this dreadful pandemic than ever before.

With heaviness in his soul he realized he could not solve this alone, for all his determination to do so. He needed new ideas, a fresh perspective. He hurried to his appointment, toward a place that might provide what he sought.

Chapter Five

Professor Altan Sibelius had some Bittersweet. Several varieties, in fact, but Valor settled for the most common extract, made from the bark and stems of the plant. In addition, the good professor had given him a seedling to add to his own nursery, in case he wished to propagate more for future experiments.

"An interesting combination, my boy," Sibelius said. Valor found it amusing that the Professor called him "boy," having no idea that Valor exceeded him in age by more than a century. "*Hamamelis virginiana* acts as an anti-inflammatory, especially effective on skin conditions and for staunching of blood flow. *Achillea Millefolium* has diuretic properties, also aiding in the clotting of blood and general expulsion of fluids. Together, they'd pack a potent punch in rendering someone resistant to say, bleeding to death. At the same time, Yarrow is often used to prevent heart attacks, which requires the opposite effect of reducing the clot response."

Valor noted Sibelius' use of Darcy's forgotten label for Witch Hazel—*Hamamelis virginiana*. The two herbs seemed to double up on a general purpose of bleeding cessation and skin problems. This made him think of Shania's facial lesions.

"Now, Bittersweet, *Solanum dulcamar,*" Sibelius continued, "That's not to be toyed with. Nightshade, you know…like Belladonna, Valerian; all toxic, and lethal in sufficient doses. The only reason to combine this with the other two would be for pain relief, I would think." The professor used his index finger to balance a pen straight up on its ballpoint tip as he considered the matter further. "Or, there is the historic use of Bittersweet in treating cancerous tumors, as well as warts, boils and other external growths." He tossed the pen flat onto the desk. "You know all this, McCaine; why come to me?"

Valor inhaled a long breath. "Just a hunch. Something a student here suggested to me. I thought it might have some merit, and wanted to investigate further. Thank you for the samples." He rose to leave.

"Not at all, dear boy. You never said what symptoms you were trying to alleviate. You have a patient with bleeding sores and tumors?"

"No. As I said, it's more of a student project. I have more far-reaching concerns. Unrelated."

Sibelius stroked his wispy gray beard. "You sure? You're here, you might as well ask all of your questions, patient-related or no. I might not be around much longer," the professor chuckled.

None of us might, Valor thought. He sat back down. "What would you suggest for…psychotherapy?" He waited for the professor's reaction.

Sibelius turned a learned eye toward him. "With herbs? Or something more," he paused. "Synthetic?"

Valor stretched his hands apart, palms up. "Whichever. What have you got?"

Sibelius made a clucking noise. "You'll have to be more specific. Psychotropic? Hallucinogen? Going out on a limb, that."

"Stimulants. Psychokinesis, ESP. Something to kick-start the brain, not impair it. I'm not looking to get high, Professor. I want to transcend the limitations of common thought."

"You don't want much, do you?" the Professor wisecracked. He shrugged and pulled a book from his well-stocked shelves. "Brain boosters, huh? If you want natural, start looking to the Chinese. Gingko biloba is the best-known. Add Ginseng to the list….several varieties there, though." He handed him the book. "But if you're looking for the wonder drug, it doesn't exist. Dopamines and norepinephrine have documented results, but you know better than I that everything has a down side. Be careful."

"I will. Thanks again."

"Wait, there's a paper I came across on the University intranet. Interesting stuff, not far off from what you've been asking about. Let me print it off."

Valor waited as Sibelius sat down at his computer with a grunt. Old age didn't sit well with anybody — Mortals or Witches. A few pages popped out of the printer, and he reached for them himself, to save the aging professor the trouble. "I'll read it over, thanks."

Sibelius waved off his gratitude. "Think nothing of it. All in the name of science, and the good of mankind, eh?" he said with a smile. "See you at the conference?"

Valor nodded. The National Alternative Medicine conference would begin in a few weeks. He'd almost forgotten. *For the good of mankind*, he repeated in his mind. For the good of all kind, he hoped. As he left the Faculty of Pharmacy, he scanned the papers he'd scooped from the printer. The article, entitled '*Blood Borne; Sanguine antigens, Curse or Cure,'* made him stop halfway down the long flight of stone steps outside the building. The author's name gave him further pause. He stared at it, ensuring he'd read it right. *Darcy M. deHavalend, Undergraduate, Faculty of Pharmacy, University of Massachussetts.*

Miss Darcy? He didn't know if Darcy had been her first name or last, and only assumed she attended the University. But her interest in pharmacology certainly fit. He would read this article with utmost interest. He slid the papers in to his messenger bag along with Professor Sibelius'gifts. The Library building stood nearby, and he headed there to continue his reading.

The Library seemed as a living thing, students and staff circulating within its aisles like blood pumping through arteries. Steady, continuous and life-giving. Valor made his way to one of the quieter corners he knew, furnished with heavy antique tables and velvet armchairs. Not the kind of modern furniture today's student with laptops and tablets seemed to favor, so the area stayed relatively unused.

He turned at the end of the 9000 section to enter his hidden enclave of library space, only to find it already occupied; and with the unlikeliest of tenants.

Miss Darcy.

She looked up at the sudden movement, staring at his knees for a split second before her eyes traveled up the height of his tall body. Her red-gold curls bounced around her freckled, pretty face as her chin tilted upward. Her lips parted open, stopped in mid-lyric of whatever music blasted through the earbuds she wore. She grasped at the thin wire leading from them to a device in her pocket and pulled. The earbuds plopped onto the pages of the open book in her lap. Round, blue eyes took him in. Funny, he hadn't remembered the color of her eyes. Like cornflowers. Soft and calming.

"Dr. McCaine?" she whispered, as if somewhat in awe of him.

"Hello, Miss Darcy. Fancy meeting you here. May I?" he asked, indicating one of the chairs next to hers. She nodded and continued to stare at him, as if he'd appeared out of thin air. He could of course, appear out of thin air; but not the sort of thing he did in public places.

"Very good to see you," he said in an appropriate library voice, and seated himself. "I didn't know you were a student here. What program are you in?"

"Sciences..." she said, holding up her book so he could see the cover. Pharmacology 101. "But I'm not Miss Darcy...I mean...yes I am, but Darcy is my first name."

"Ah," he said, tilting his head back a bit. "Well, let's start over then, shall we?" He extended his hand to her. "Valor McCaine."

Her hand reached out and grasped his. "Darcy deHavalend. Thank you for your help the other day...I was planning to call the shop tomorrow." Her small hand felt chilled. He wanted to keep hold of it, warm it. He sensed she needed protection in some way. He let her be the first to break contact, and she released his hand with a nervous smile.

"I can save you the trip, Miss Darcy. Would you mind if I continued to call you that? I like it."

Darcy dropped her blue eyes in a gesture of embarrassment. "Just Darcy would be fine."

Valor smiled. "All right." He reached in to his messenger bag for the extract of Bittersweet. "Solanum dulcamara," he said, handing her the tiny tincture bottle. "I presume you know it's a narcotic."

She took the bottle, cradling it with both hands. "Thank you. Yes. I can't pay you for it right now," she apologized. "I have the money, just not with me. I would have brought it to the store..." Her voice faded off, and she swallowed uncomfortably. "I'm not going to use it for myself, to get high or anything. Just so you know."

He shook his head. "Don't worry about it. I think I have an idea of what you're going to use it for." He produced the printed article and showed it to her. "Would this be you, then?"

If she'd been nervous in his presence before, her reddening face confirmed it now. She squinched her eyes shut. "You read my paper?"

Valor leaned his elbow on the armrest of his chair and plopped his chin in his hand as he regarded her in contained amusement. "Some of it. Look at me."

Her cornflower-blue eyes popped open.

"I'm going to finish reading it right now. Will you stay here while I do?"

She blinked. "Uh, sure."

"I may have questions. Will you answer them?"

She held the medicine bottle in one hand while twisting her earbud wires in loops with the other. "If you'll answer some of mine."

He tipped his chin in agreement, turned his attention to the papers and began to read. Darcy fidgeted, trying to fit her tangled earbuds into her ears and focus on the book in her lap while she waited.

In a few minutes, Valor set the paper down.

"Darcy. I think we have some things to discuss. Over dinner. Are you free this evening?"

*

"Don't you want to live forever?"

Lucie felt the hairs stand up on her neck, and the stony points of the brick wall behind her digging painfully into her skin. Germayne's power held her fast and hard against it, without moving so much as an earlobe to cast the spell.

"Don't you," he said, not as a question.

Lucie gritted her teeth. "Not with you…" A sharp pain delivered to her gut with a mere glance from Germayne cut her words short. She cast her eyes away from him, clamping her mouth shut for the moment. The alley smelled of cat urine, garbage and car exhaust. Fuck her bastard cousin! His years away hadn't taught him any humility, or even wisdom, in her opinion. He was as blinded by power and cruelty as ever. Worse than ever, judging by this new aura of megalomania that surrounded him.

"I know you didn't mean that," he responded. "I can feel you weakening with every second that passes. You want me to help you. You want your powers back, yes you do. I'm the *only* one who can help you, you know that. Not that loose-dicked doctor."

"Valor helps me. In ways you can't imagine. I thought you liked him, you were close once."

Germayne's lips contorted into a foul grin. "He's stupid. Never sees the bigger picture, the dumb fuck. Ruled by his cock." He snorted a laugh. "Just like you, eh cuz?"

"You only wish you had a cock like his," Lucie countered. "Bet yours is like your brain, shriveled and poisonous…. aagh!" Another of Germayne's psychic blows wracked her body, making her bite her tongue and squeeze her eyes shut in agony.

"You will help me get to him. I guarantee it."

Lucie jerked her head side to side. "Why should I help you? Do your own dirty work. Leave me out of it."

"Why, you ask? Obvious, isn't it? Without me, you die. It's that simple. Now take me to him."

Lucie met Germayne's eyes, focusing all her will and her hatred upon him to gain strength. Her fingernails scratched the rough brick beneath her palms, and in a last desperate rally of her powers, disappeared into the wall at her back.

Chapter Six

Darcy waited in front of the Commonwealth Bookshop near the corner of Milk and Washington in downtown Boston. Valor had promised to meet her at 6:00pm to escort her to dinner. Apparently, the location of his favorite restaurant was too obscure for directions. It also seemed curious that he hadn't offered to pick her up. A successful doctor must at least drive a decent car. Oh well, it wasn't like a date or anything; just two scientific minds collaborating.

The not-so-secret part of her wished it were more, though. Seeing him sitting next to her this afternoon, chin in hand, fixing her with those fabulous eyes, had sent thrills rocketing through her whole body. It took all of her strength to sit still while he'd read her essay. She couldn't wait to ask him questions, and couldn't imagine what questions he might have for her. She'd written the *Blood Borne* whitepaper as a freshman, mostly entertaining her own frustrations about diseases and heredity, especially as it related to her family.

She looked in all directions down the intersecting streets for any sign of the handsome Dr. McCaine. Two minutes past six. He didn't seem the type to be late. She hugged her knee-

length beige cardigan around herself as the air grew chilly.
Not having a wide choice, she departed from her standard
attire of jeans and a zip-hoodie for this evening and wore the
best her wardrobe currently offered — a white long-sleeved
blouse and a black skirt. She looked down at her unpainted
toenails peeking out from wedge-heeled black sandals, the
only 'dress' shoes she owned.

"Hello, Darcy."

She jumped as Valor McCaine touched her elbow in
greeting. She hadn't seen him approach, and she'd been
watching for quite awhile. How'd he sneak up on her like
that?

"You look lovely. I hope you're hungry…shall we?" he
said, taking a firmer grip on her elbow and guiding her down
the sidewalk.

Darcy appreciated his compliment, knowing full well
she wasn't lovely at all. Just a poor, frumpy student doing
the best she could. She didn't deserve to be seen with the
classiest, smartest, not to mention hottest, man in the city.
Yet here she stood, going to dinner with him. His *kathra*
smelled strong, and now that she knew it, the scent came
readily to her; intoxicating. The dreamlike sensation she'd
experienced earlier returned. She hadn't been affected by
anyone's *kathra* this way before…what made this man so
unusual?

They walked a block or so when Valor came to a stop at
the entrance to a side street. With a slow nod of his head, he
gestured to the left. "That way," he said. They turned into
a narrow, nondescript lane that had no discernible shops or
businesses at first glance. Suddenly, Darcy noticed a string of
glowing yellow bulbs over an archway a few meters down.

"Oh," she said. "Kinda off the beaten path, isn't it?"

"Trust me?" Valor said with a big smile, and for a

moment she thought she might melt into the cobblestones at their feet. She smiled back and nodded.

He led her into the little establishment that bore no name over the doorway or on a sign of any kind. Immediate warmth and relaxation settled over her as they stepped inside. The place seemed to overflow with welcome and good cheer, the delicious aromas of fresh bread and baked pasta swirling in the air like smoke. A rotund gentleman in a striped burgundy suit bustled over to them.

"My friend, so good to see you," the man gushed, slapping Valor on the shoulder. "Where have you been hiding? You've lost weight...come, eat!"

"Good to see you as well, Rosario. I've been busy, that's all. Table for two, please."

"Of course," Rosario said, and turned to address Darcy. "Welcome, mademoiselle. The good doctor, as always, has excellent taste." He gave a bow and gestured to a corner table flanked by two adjacent windows. Funny. She hadn't seen any windows from the outside. She followed Rosario, walking ahead of Valor.

When they were seated, Darcy glanced around the room. The place seemed busy for a weeknight, and in such an out of the way location. Rosario reappeared and poured wine for them.

"What would you like?" Valor asked.

"Uh," Darcy began, looking down at the empty table between them. "Probably a menu," she laughed.

A wry smile grew on the doctor's face. "No menus here. Just say what you want, and they'll bring it."

Darcy shifted in her chair. Not awkward enough, being in an unfamiliar restaurant with a heart-stopping stud for a date. Now she had to try and think up a dish that wouldn't expose her unrefined tastes in food? *Ugh.* He waited patiently for her answer. All that came to mind was some of her grandmother's specialties that she remembered appearing on the dinner table with a snap of her grandma's fingers. "Cornish hen with wild rice stuffing," she said.

Valor gave a satisfactory nod. "Sounds great. I'll have the same." He raised his glass of wine, indicating for her follow. She picked up the delicate, long-stemmed glass and raised it to her lips. She turned 21 on her last birthday, but Valor hadn't even asked if she was of age. Did he care? Rosario certainly hadn't seemed concerned. She took a sip, and wasn't sure if it were the atmosphere, or just his company, but it seemed like the best-tasting wine in the world.

"I think we have something in common," Valor said. "After reading your essay, we seem to be looking for the same thing."

For a wishful second, Darcy thought the doctor might be coming on to her. But he seemed all business again. That is why she came here, she reminded herself. "Oh? What in particular caught your attention?" She moved her hands to her lap, out of sight from the tabletop, so he couldn't see her twisting her fingers in anxiety.

"Your observations about blood antigens, and how they are passed down genetically. Specifically, your conjecture that the genetic path could be…interrupted, with the introduction of the right bio-agents. Your herbal compounds, I'm guessing?"

Darcy cringed remembering this morning's disastrous test results. She looked up at him with hopelessness in her eyes, not sure how to begin describing the situation. The arrival of dinner saved her from further explanation.

Rosario set the plates in front of them with a flourish, his appearance every bit as sudden as with the wine. She hadn't heard Valor give him their order, but two perfectly roasted game hens with wild rice stuffing now graced their table, exactly as she remembered her grandma presenting them.

Something seemed both very right, and very wrong, with this restaurant. "This is amazing," she said, inhaling the delicious aroma of the food. Her hunger got the best of her, and she carved into the roast fowl with gusto.

They ate without much more conversation, as Darcy occupied her mouth with bite after bite of delicious fare and gulps of wine. She couldn't recall eating so much in so short a time. Months of student austerity must have heightened her appetite. With her plate clean, she dabbed her mouth with a napkin, and emptied her wineglass to wash down the last of her meal. She stopped in mid-slurp, noticing how Dr. McCaine stared at her. God, where were her table manners? She felt like Oliviah, gorging herself at her bowl.

"Excuse me," she said, polishing off the last drops of wine. "I...guess I haven't tasted anything so good in a long time. Do you come here often? Must be one of Boston's best-kept secrets."

He continued to regard her with his smoldering violet gaze. "You could say that, yes. I come here occasionally. You like it, then?"

Self-conscious over her empty plate that looked as though Oliviah had licked it clean, Darcy dropped the napkin on top of it. "Yes. Thank you." With nothing further to procrastinate with, she launched into her troubles. "About my herbal compounds. I have some data imaging I need you to look at. Not very promising, though. Would you mind?"

Valor's expression intensified. "Not at all. Please," he said, gesturing for her to continue. She reached into her sling bag for her tablet and called up the digital images from the lab microscope. He swiped through them, tilting his head a little as he viewed each new image. "What are we seeing here? What are the control elements?"

Darcy cleared her throat, wishing for a little more wine to smooth it out. "A failed experiment, I'm afraid. I didn't have the *Solanum dulcamara* so I prepared a serum of *millefolia* and…."

"*Hammemelus virginiana*," Valor supplied.

"Yes. The test cells are from two different subjects, both affected with a debilitating disorder." The best way she could describe it without going into too much detail. "I don't understand how the results could vary so wildly. Have you seen anything like it before?"

Valor concentrated on the visuals for several moments. "Astonishing rate of mitosis…that's crazy."

"I'll say," Darcy concurred. "It nearly blew up my kitchen…I mean, my laboratory."

"Your laboratory's in your kitchen?"

"More like my kitchen's in my laboratory. There's more test tubes and flasks than there are pots and pans."

He smirked at this, but kept his eyes on the tablet screen. His *kathra* began to elevate. Darcy could tell he'd found something deeply disturbing about her data. He handed the tablet back to her.

"Miss Darcy. I think we should join forces on this. You may not realize what you're dealing with."

She swallowed hard. The doctor recognized something? A spark of hope lit her brain, but at the same time she grew fearful of having to reveal the whole story to a stranger, whether drawn to him romantically or not. What would he think about a family of…for lack of a better word…witches?

"May I see your laboratory?" he asked.

Darcy's heart jumped. My God, he could be in her apartment. Near her bed and everything. *Holy shit*. She wanted another sip of wine, but remembered she'd finished it. She looked down at her glass, and inexplicably found it refilled of the rich, fruity libation.

"If you insist."

*

Shania had difficulty breathing. She lay shivering on
Dr. McCaine's examining table, her nude body wrapped
in the sheets and blankets from the guest room bed. Her
lungs rasped with the effort of inhaling and exhaling, the
facial lesions forming and festering on her skin again.
Though Valor had left food and drink for her, she hadn't
partaken of either. She needed her fix of Germayne's drug
concoction more than she needed sustenance. Sweat covered
her forehead and torso, despite her chills. Her long flaxen
hair clung in wet strands around her throat and trailed down
her back. She huddled there on the soft divan, awaiting the
doctor's return.

Lightning flashed outside, followed by rumbling thunder
that shook the windowpanes. Rain pelted down, drumming a
frantic melody on the roof. She cast her glazed eyes around
the room, as though searching for something. Another blaze
of light at the window caught her attention and she jerked
her fevered head toward it. She trembled and could not turn
away from the glass, where a pair of evil yellow eyes stared
in at her.

She screamed and raked her hands over her face, grasping
at the wet sheets to shield herself from the dreadful entity
hovering at the window.

"You are mine," came a voice, even louder than the
thunder outside. "You cannot hide. You will be punished."
Shania's body slid onto the floor, her legs thrashing against
the folds of bedcovers wrapped around her. With her hands at
her throat, she clawed at some invisible force that threatened
to choke the life from her.

Chapter Seven

LuSie von Pecht paced the halls of the Witches Consulate, her stiletto heels clacking against the rough-hewn floor stones, deep in thought. Her cousin's return had caught her off-guard, and she didn't feel safe returning to her home after their meeting in the coffee shop. She'd tried to walk away and act as though his threats meant nothing to her, only to have him trap her in that alley, revealing the true depth of his insanity.

Added to his considerable weaponry, insanity provided gasoline to an already out of control fire. Did she believe he had the cure for the insidious malady that had taken Artizia and countless others? She wasn't certain, but couldn't afford to call his bluff either. He and Valor had been partners once, in a way. Considerably the elder, Germayne played the part of mentor to Valor all those years ago. What had gone wrong between them she didn't know. Only that Artizia's death spurred a falling out and they hadn't spoken since. Germayne had disappeared shortly afterward.

Though accustomed to her cousin's outlandish style, his newest plans frightened her beyond anything he'd ever cooked up before. Still, the possibility of a cure, of staying beautiful and powerful forever, dangled tantalizingly before her.

She did not want to die.

If Germayne truly held that power, his plan was foolproof. Those who wished to live must align with him and swear fealty. The rest would die by some manifestation of this monstrous sickness. Yet, he needed Valor. What did Valor have, that Germayne so desperately required? Enough that he'd be willing to kill her if she didn't help him get it?

She loved Valor. There, she'd said it. No power on earth or otherworld would make her betray him. There had to be a way to save herself and yet spare Valor, too. She had to warn him.

*

Darcy led Valor up the stairs of her apartment building. She felt a tad giddy after all that delicious wine, and more than a little frisky. But he'd asked to see her laboratory, and what better opportunity to get him alone? Her trepidations about his age had somehow vanished during dinner.

They reached the second floor landing, and she fumbled with her key to get in. As usual, Oliviah vaulted out the door, but didn't make it down the hall. Instead, Valor caught the animal in midair and held her writhing paws and tail close to his chest until she simmered down.

"Who might this be?" he asked, clutching the calico furball firmly in his sculpted hands.

"That's Oliviah. Quick, bring her inside. The landlord doesn't know about her."

The three of them slipped inside and Darcy bolted the door out of habit. Valor lowered Oliviah to the floor, where she promptly shot across the room and leapt to the windowsill. She hissed in indignation at both of them.

"Ignore her," Darcy said. "Well. This is it. This is home."

"It's nice. It suits you." He laid his coat on the arm of the worn sofa. It had come with the place, Darcy having no input as to its color or quality.

"Thanks. Kitchen's this way," she swept her arm in that direction. The doctor looked with interest over the collection of scientific tools and gadgets that littered her limited counter space. He opened the little refrigerator that dominated the area, peered in, and closed it again. The Styrofoam incubator had been left in place and he checked that too.

"Is this where you incubated the samples I saw?"

"Uh-huh. I had to throw out the dishes, they were beyond saving."

"I see. Show me exactly what you did."

Darcy showed him the herbal mixtures and their proportions, the blood samples and the cultures in which they grew, her notes on time, temperatures and quantities. She described the resulting growth that had woken her and Oliviah that morning, and pointed to the ceiling.

The hideous blob still clung to the surface, and as they looked up, the drip that had been hanging from it finally gave way and fell, landing on the doctor's chin.

"Oh, my God!" Darcy howled, snapping off a sheet of paper towel from the roll by the sink. "Oh, that's so gross… .I'm so sorry, here…" She stepped in close to him and wiped the disgusting substance from his face. Her hand cupped his jaw as she made two or three passes with the towel, making sure she'd gotten all of it. "Are you okay, jeez I'm sorry… yuck. That's horrible, that's…" she stopped talking, unable to think of any more apologies.

Without warning, his arm slipped around her waist. He caught her upraised hand that held the now-crumpled paper towel by the wrist and tipped his face downward to meet hers. She felt his breath on her cheek and the scent of his *kathra* filling her nostrils, intense and laced with a new thread that throbbed with emotion.

"Darcy…" he whispered hoarsely. "Forgive me." Then his lips were upon hers, hungry and searching. Her body trembled, but returned his kiss with equal fervor. Boldly, she slipped her tongue into his mouth, entwining with his as they explored each other. Her breasts tingled, swelling with her heated blood as they pressed against him.

He broke their kiss, but didn't release his hold on her. "I'm sorry. You weren't prepared for that," he whispered into her hair as he rested his chin on top of her curly head.

"How do you know?" she whispered back. "Maybe I've been prepared for that since the day I walked into your pharmacy."

He chuckled, and stroked her hair. "Okay. Maybe I'm the one who wasn't prepared. I should know better, taking advantage of you like this."

She snuggled into his chest, breathing deeply of his *kathra* as it modulated and settled down. "It feels right, to me."

He lowered his arms to wrap around her body, holding her firm. Neither spoke for several moments, their silence communicating what words could not. Darcy thought if one perfect moment could be preserved forever, suspended like air bubbles in blown crystal, this would be it.

Loud meows and the push of a furry body rubbing against her legs shattered the crystal image in her mind.

"The jig's up," Valor said, watching Oliviah's sinuous dance between his calves and her yellow eyes staring sweetly at the two of them. Darcy swished her away with one impatient foot.

"Hey, watch it! I like him, too. Why should you get all the attention around here?"

"Beat it," she replied hastily.

"She's alright. I like cats." Valor released her to rest both hands on her shoulders and look into her eyes. "Tell me, what were you hoping to discover with those tests?"

Uh-oh. She wouldn't be able to solve a thing without telling him the whole truth. Besides, from his comments over dinner, he clearly knew something she didn't. Knowledge she needed. "A formula to slow the growth of the infected cells, of course. But it failed, as you saw. What did you mean when you said, "you may not realize what you're dealing with?""

He searched her eyes, as if judging her fit to hear his next words. "The infectious agent is a virus, one I've been researching for quite some time. It only affects certain types of individuals, and is lethal in most cases. If it's spreading, I need to know about it. Darcy…" he paused. "Whose blood samples are those?"

Darcy swallowed hard. Lethal? He'd just confirmed her worst fears.

"My mother and grandmother."

Valor's jaw ground side to side as he considered her words. "What are their symptoms?"

"I…I'm, not sure I can tell you," she stammered, shaking her head.

"You have to, this is more serious than you know. Be a scientist, now."

Perhaps she could reveal some of it without sounding crazy. "My mom, she seems to have a deteriorating skin condition. She's only 45, and looks more like my grandmother, who is 70. As if the aging process has been accelerated somehow."

"And your grandmother, she appears her natural age? Are there other symptoms?"

Darcy felt tears building, and dropped her eyes. This wasn't going to be easy. "She looks her age. But she's nearly an invalid now, and can't do a lot of things. Special things, that she's been doing all her life."

The doctor tilted his head. "That doesn't sound unusual. Most of us lose abilities as we age. There's more to this, what else?"

"Dr. McCaine," she said, her voice shaky. You have to promise you'll not repeat this. And you have to promise you will take me seriously."

He nodded. "Go on."

"My family…is not normal. I've known this all along, I never needed to discuss it before. My mom, and my grandma too, have psychokinetic abilities. They…can make things grow. Make objects appear and disappear. They can speak to me telepathically, and transport themselves over long distances. But now they're sick. I'm afraid they'll die when they lose these gifts." She turned her blue eyes upward again to meet his intense violet ones that now seemed to darken with her revelation.

"These gifts," he repeated. "That's not all they will lose if they've contracted the virus."

Darcy's face fell. "What are you saying?"

"What are you *not* saying, Darcy deHavalend? Are you not worried how it might affect you? I told you the virus, so far, only affects certain individuals. And the predisposition appears to be hereditary." He stroked his hands down the length of her arms and clasped her hands. "What are you?"

She shook her head in a motion of denial. "I don't know. We never spoke the word, but some called us…Witches."

Valor tilted his face toward her in a slow nod. "Witches." Taking a deep breath, he continued. "The virus has a name, because I gave it a name. Némesati. It's been around a long time, like me. And it only affects Witchkind. For a moment I thought it might be spreading to mortals, from what you

said. That's one comfort, I suppose. It's still confined to…
our kind.

"What kind are you?" she asked, barely able to speak the
words. Her hands squeezed his.

"I'm a Warlock. And a good one hundred and fifty years
older than you."

Darcy sniffed back the remnants of her earlier tears and
threw him a steady, brave gaze. "I like older men. Will my
age, or lack of it, be a barrier for us?"

Valor smiled and squeezed her hand in return. "Only if we
let it." He glanced around at her jury-rigged laboratory. "I
think we should move your experiments to bigger quarters.
Better resources, easier to work collaboratively. Would you
mind continuing your research in my office?"

Oliviah had found her way onto the countertop and
launched herself to land on the doctor's shoulders, wrapping
her tail beneath his chin. Valor barely flinched, and reached
up to stroke her silky, spotted coat.

"Only if you take me, too."

Darcy smiled. "Would you mind being a walking, talking
scratching post?"

"I've been worse," he said.

Chapter Eight

Valor returned home after arranging that Darcy would bring her things the next evening, after classes. He could not explain even to himself the dangerous attraction he felt for this young...what? Half-witch? He'd kissed her on impulse, but had to summon all his gentlemanly skills to keep his hands off her. It bordered on indecent, his feelings for her, and they amplified his regret and longing for his lost Artizia. What did that make him? Unfaithful? A philanderer? He'd been with countless women between then and now, and not one of them had meant anything to him. Somehow, this girl made him uncomfortable with that.

He entered the back door, noticing nothing unusual until he stepped on broken glass scattered about the threshold. The glass panes in the door were intact, indicating the shards must have came from elsewhere. The floor above? He cursed himself for leaving Shania unattended for so long.

Up the stairs he raced, hoping to find her peacefully asleep in his guest bed. He reached the top floor. Icy blasts of cold air whistled through the rooms. Every window in sight lay shattered, leaving nothing but gaping, unshielded holes in the framework of the house. "Shania!"

He crossed over to the guest room, more glass crunching beneath the soles of his shoes, only to find the bed unoccupied with the sheets and blankets missing. Curtains billowed at the window as the wind howled in from outside. "Shania," he called again, returning to the main room that served as his office and examination area. There, he saw her hunched form lying underneath his examining table. Her bare feet protruded from the twisted bedsheets that bound the rest of her body like a straightjacket.

Reaching her side, he dropped to a crouch and eased her onto her back. His lips formed a tight line as he looked her over, the oozing sores again covering not only her face, but her neck, chest and arms as well. "Shania," he said gently. "I'm sorry I left you, are you all right? Please talk to me."

Her body felt limp and lifeless as he raised her to sitting position, resting her head against his shoulder. He could see she still breathed, but sensed other vital signs near failing. Her condition had been stable when he left…what the hell had happened here?

He lifted her from the floor and carried her into the bathroom. In the bright light overhead, he saw the red blotches had spread to her legs as well, and a harsh, purplish bruising blossomed around her throat. He laid her out in the tub, loosening the sodden sheets from around her and summoning running water from the taps with a wave of his hand. As he smoothed the warm water, infused with Yarrow and Witch Hazel, over her ravaged skin, she began to regain consciousness, uttering frail moans amid uneven breathing.

Steam rose into the air, clouding the small space with aromatic vapor from the herbal essences. "Shania," he said again. "What happened?"

She jerked to alertness, grasping at Valor's arms and dousing him with bathwater in the process. "Help me! He'll kill me, please…help me!" Valor bore down on her, keeping her thrashing limbs in check while trying to understand what had transpired.

"Calm down, it's all right, you're safe now," he shouted above the splashing water and Shania's yelps. "Tell me what happened!"

Her struggling ceased as she focused on Valor's face. Her eyes looked dark and hollowed, and she fixed him with a piteous gaze that brought his feelings of protectiveness and outrage at her attacker to the surface.

"Germayne was here," she squeaked, and began to shake uncontrollably. "Oh, Valor. He wants you...he demands to see you. He'll kill me if you don't go to him. Please... do something. Give me something...I'll die if you don't. Please." She clung to him, soaking him with water from the bath, her voice dissolving into wracking sobs.

"Shhh..." he soothed. He knew now, by her condition and her pleas that she suffered from a drug addiction. He suspected it the moment she'd landed on his doorstep. "I will see him, and he will pay for what he's done to you. Quiet now, I'm sorry I wasn't here to protect you. I won't leave you alone again."

"Promise..." she said, in between coughing spasms.

"I promise." With that promise, came a resignation that fate had caught up with him at last. He had unfinished business to attend.

*

Tracking Germayne's movements wasn't easy. The morning following her encounter with him, Lucie faced the fact that she was not on top of her game, and had no way of telling what tricks, formulas or knowledge Germayne may have acquired, studied or stolen from others during his absence.

She'd traced his path from the coffee shop to a shopping

mall, to a hotel complex downtown, and the University stadium. None of these locations made any sense to her, and detected no special activity on his part at any of them. Now, she paced along the terrace of a warehouse building near Boston Harbor. From this vantage point, she could see the many docks from which tankers, cargo containers, military vessels and fishing trawlers arrived and departed. She found the smell irritating. All that human and animal traffic combined with the odors of fuels and machinery. Disgusting.

She watched Germayne board a particular craft; a large, sophisticated-looking boat of private origin. More like a giant yacht than anything else. Alongside the call letters she could make out a name – the Pandora I. It appeared Germayne made some friends in high places. She laughed at herself. Germayne had no friends. He had captives.

He'd been in there for more than half an hour, with no visible crewmembers nor movement on deck. The wind off the waterfront brought more of the foul aromas to her nostrils, along with a distinct chill. She thought about conjuring up a hot toddy for herself if her quarry stayed out of sight much longer.

She shifted her feet to keep moving, looking down at her toes and thinking about a nice fur cape instead of a hot toddy. Wouldn't take much, a simple spell really…no one around to witness. Oh hell, what she'd really prefer was another appointment with Valor to keep warm; she missed the sexy bastard already. It had been four days since they'd had sex. Next time, she would wrap her lips around his impressive cock and suck him until he begged for mercy. She imagined his hands all over her tits, squeezing and fondling, pinching her nipples.

In mid-fantasy, a horrendous boom sounded from the direction of the harbor, jolting Lucie back to the present and nearly to the ground as she lost her balance. She gaped in horror as she saw the yacht in which Germayne visited explode in multiple bursts of flame. Pillars of smoke mushroomed into the air above, and the sound reverberated with such power she had to cover her ears.

She crouched on the concrete terrace, peering through the metal railing at the horrific sight and her mind raced as to the significance of this event. Did Germayne cause the explosion, disapparating before detonation? To what purpose? Or was it a freak accident, killing everyone aboard? *Could it be that simple*? she thought, the most dangerous warlock in the world, dead by accident?

Either way, Germayne would not be seen coming out. The explosion put the surrounding vessels in jeopardy and triggered a massive emergency response, fire trucks and security vehicles rushing to the scene. Lucie scrambled to her feet, closing her eyes to the destruction and focusing on her next move…to tell Valor. She disapparated, leaving empty space on the terrace where she once stood, and materialized in front of McCaine's Pharmacy.

Not cool, appearing on the front street in broad daylight. But in her agitation she did not much care. The neon sign glowed OPEN, and she hurried inside. A few customers looked her way but she ignored them, scanning the room for Valor. He stood between the rows of pharmacy supplies behind the counter. Her rapid approach made enough noise that he faced front and caught sight of her.

"Lucie?"

She hoped she didn't look as frightened as she felt. She placed her gloved hands flat on the counter to stop their trembling and leaned toward him. "Valor. I need to speak with you. Now."

He moved out from the back shop to greet her, a dimpled grin forming on his face. "We don't have an appointment until next week, Lu. Can't wait, huh?"

She let out an exasperated breath, and lowered her
voice to a whisper. "Ordinarily I'd say yes. That's not it…I
need to speak to you in private." She glanced toward the
remaining patrons browsing the store. Valor considered
her for a moment, then cast a suggestive spell with a subtle
motion of his wrist. Everyone turned to the exit, replaced any
merchandise they held to the shelves and walked out without
a word.

"What is it, Lu?"

"You're in danger. Germayne is back, and he's looking
for you."

Valor nodded. "Yes I know."

"Do you? Do you know why?"

"Not really, just that he's demanding to see me. He should
know how to find me, though." Valor swept his hand across
the expanse of empty shop. "Don't know why he hasn't just
turned up."

Lucie found his calmness alarming. Valor of all people
knew the depths of Germayne's power and depravity. "Well,
I do. He says he has the cure for…what killed Artizia and all
the others. He says all of us will contract the virus and die,
unless we align with him."

He looked at Lucie blankly. "Lu. I know he has the
cure. I've always known. He had it long ago, before he
disappeared. And he chose not to share it."

Lucie's eyes widened. "That's when you stopped working
together."

He looked away from her, out into the street through the
shop window. "He could have saved her, Lu. He could have
saved everyone, the selfish bastard."

They stood there in silence, calculating the meaning of
Germayne's actions. Then Lucie fished out the Horse Head
token she'd kept from the Dragonchess match and placed it

on the counter. "Well, there's something missing from his plans. Whatever it is, he needs you."

Valor scoffed. "The pandemic is spreading, and the virus may be mutating. It's looking like I need him, too. So we may as well have our little showdown now. Where is he?"

Lucie bit her lip. "That's the problem. I've been following him, trying to figure out his plan. I tracked him to Boston Harbor just now, and he boarded a ship that blew to smithereens in front of my eyes." She paused for effect. "He might be dead."

Chapter Nine

Professor Sibelius packed his briefcase in preparation for the National Alternative Medicine conference only a few days away. He had all the dissertations and research papers for the plenary and session speakers printed and sorted into presentation folders for his reference. Of particular interest, a session on Nootropics and brain tachometry would be presented on day 2 of the conference. He found himself returning to his conversation with Dr. McCaine earlier in the week.

The enhancement of brain function was a long-discussed topic in his field. Some scientists held the belief that humans only engaged about ten percent of their brain capacity in daily life, and that the remaining 90 percent represented an untapped, unexplored resource of unmatched potential. But how to awaken this sleeping giant? That remained controversial.

Dr. McCaine had come ostensibly for naturopathic counsel. Medicinal uses of herbs dated back countless centuries, some of it substantiated with consistent, measurable findings. The rest, well, sometimes the belief in the cure was just as effective as the cure itself, even when none existed. The other train of thought on how to expand the mind led to narcotics and manufactured drugs. He worried that McCaine might be dabbling in something deeper than he let on. A student project? Seemed a little trippy, in Sibelius' opinion. He was no stranger to psychotropics himself. After all, he'd lived through the Seventies, too.

On a big campus like U of M, the use of neuro-enhancers and "smart drugs" ran rampant. It would be all too easy for McCaine, or anyone else for that matter, to score these types of substances. So far, no experiments he knew of involved a combination of herbal and clinical stimulants. That is, no others aside from his own. He decided he'd keep an eye on Dr. McCaine at the conference, pay attention to what sessions he attended and maybe tag along to a few.

*

Darcy couldn't decide whether to mix the Bittersweet serum now, or wait until she'd moved her equipment to Dr. McCaine's office. In her anxiety to discover if her original formula would work, she wanted to do it right away. But the doctor's office would have more space, more tools, more resources. It made sense to wait. On the other hand, the control conditions might be altered by moving to new digs.

"Oliviah," she called. The yellow-eyed feline strolled into view. "What do you think? Should I do the experiment now, or wait?"

"You're asking my opinion?" Oliviah's mouth opened into one of those gaping cat-yawns, then wiped at her whiskers with one paw. *"Since when?"*

Darcy sighed. "Are you going to answer me or not?"

Oliviah settled into a sitting position. *"Does it matter? You're just going to do what you want, anyway."*

"Don't get snotty with me. You're always giving me your opinion whether I ask for it or not. Now's your chance… speak up."

The cat crawled into Darcy's lap and stared at her, eyes unblinking. *"Okay. You're crazy about the man. I don't know why you're wasting one more minute in this dump."*

"Dump? How dare you!" Darcy said in mock indignation. "Don't get carried away. It's not like he's asked me to move in with him." She stroked Oliviah's head, then scratched under her ears. "But I am crazy about him. Or maybe just crazy in general. Oh, Oliviah, am I doing the right thing? Do I even have a chance? Maybe I'm just a…dalliance. How do I know he doesn't make a habit of kissing young female students? How do I know there aren't hundreds of them in his little black…Blackberry…or whatever?"

Oliviah uncurled herself and stepped off Darcy's lap to take a long, lazy cat stretch. *"A little late to worry about that now. Taxi's here."* With that, the door buzzer sounded. Darcy jumped. Had Dr. McCaine ordered a taxi for her? How thoughtful…but she wasn't packed yet! She answered the buzzer, confirming that it was indeed a taxi, and asked the driver to give her five minutes.

In less than four minutes, she climbed into the cab along with her mini-fridge, incubator, and a cardboard box full of flasks, tubes, clamps and thermometers. Oliviah made it into the back seat just before the door slammed, missing her tail by only a centimeter.

"Hey!" Darcy exclaimed. "Who invited you?"

"He did. Didn't you know? He can speak to animals, too. He just doesn't have to be vocal about it, like some people I know."

Darcy rolled her eyes as she gave the address to the cabbie and they pulled away from the curb. Just what she needed. A telepathic, blabbermouth cat to tell the Hot Doc all her secrets.

When they arrived at McCaine's Pharmacy, dusk had settled in. "Fare's taken care of, Miss," the driver said. "Have a good evening."

"Thank you," Darcy said, but her attention fixed on a strange figure outside of the pharmacy's front door. A dark-haired woman dressed in a flowing cape stood there, eyeing up the taxicab as it slowed to a stop. Her dark curls, with streaks of gray, hung across her brow and dangled in ringlets on either side of her face. Her painted lips were a shocking shade of red that reflected bright as a stop light in the gathering dark.

Darcy reached for her things, Oliviah darting over her to be first out the door. As she pushed the handle down and prepared to get out, she looked up at the storefront again. The woman had disappeared as if Darcy had only imagined her, and in the same space stood Valor McCaine. He smiled in greeting and approached the vehicle.

"Let me help you with all that," he said, taking the refrigerator and Styrofoam crate from her. Oliviah leaped from the cab, landing at Valor's feet and doing her customary figure eight around his legs. He led them inside the shop and up the back stairs.

Darcy never imagined her next visit to the pharmacy would be into the private life of its owner, and she couldn't think of anyplace she'd rather be. They set up her equipment in his office, quite a long room with his desk and cabinets at one end and plenty of counter space at the other equipped with sinks, instruments, task lighting and power outlets.

Darcy prepared the modified batch of formula to include the bittersweet, and placed them in culture dishes. When she went to retrieve the blood samples, Valor stopped her.

"We should test some of yours, too. Roll up your sleeve."

He indicated one of two stools behind the counter where she obediently sat down. She pinched the cuffs of her sleeve into folds, exposing her left forearm. Valor tied a rubber tourniquet just above her elbow. Even this clinical touch sent sensual tremors up Darcy's spine, which promptly rebounded straight to her crotch. Trying to work with the man would not be easy. She'd be dropping her pants at the slightest provocation if these urges continued.

He daubed her protruding vein with alcohol from a cotton puff, and inserted the syringe. Darcy winced as she always did when having blood taken, but instead of looking away she focused on the shiny needle where it pierced her skin and watched the dark fluid fill the reservoir. In some weird way she felt a precious surrender, a blood bond of sorts, transpiring between them as he collected her sample. Her gaze drifted upward. He glanced up to meet her eyes for a half-second. It became another of those blown-crystal moments — Darcy feeling lost inside those twin oceans of violet perfection and wishing she might float adrift in their depths for eternity.

He returned his focus to the syringe, slipping the second reservoir into place and releasing the tourniquet to let the blood flow ebb. In a blink, he withdrew the sharp point from her arm and pressed the cotton ball to the puncture site. He placed a tape strip over the cotton and bent her elbow 90 degrees, indicating she should hold it there.

Valor prepared a third culture dish and injected the three blood samples in sequence. Darcy recorded the details on her tablet while he placed the cultures into a proper incubator that occupied a corner of his well-appointed lab area. When they'd finished, they sat facing each other on the lab stools.

"This could be the start of a new medical partnership. Like Banting and Best," Darcy joked. "Or Myers and Briggs."

Valor laughed. "Banting and Best were two men. And Myers and Briggs were two women. I don't think that describes us."

Darcy cocked her head back and forth. "Okay. How about Masters and Johnson?"

Valor's eyebrows went up and his lips pursed into a teasing pout. "Miss Darcy. What are you suggesting?" His tone came across as scolding, but his eyes glittered in flirtation. "We've only just met."

Darcy smiled in the wickedest way, her last vestiges of caution crumbling to ruin. She moved from her seat and stepped toward him, swinging one leg, then the other, over his thighs to sit on him as he perched on his stool. Her arms snaked around his neck and brought herself nose to nose with him. "Have we?" she purred. "Sometimes I get the feeling we've met before, don't you?" She could feel his cock hardening beneath her ass as she wriggled in tight against him.

"Mmmm..." he murmured, but did not answer. His hands smoothed over the tops of her thighs and around to her buttocks, rubbing her round cheeks in slow circles. "Young lady," he said in a low voice, laden with emotion. You are playing with fire. You don't have any idea what you may be letting yourself in for."

Darcy's stomach fluttered, matching the vibrations beginning between her legs. She agreed she did not know what lay ahead if she continued down this path. But following it did not even rank as a question anymore. Her course had already been set. "I've already let myself in," she responded in a shaky whisper. "The question is, will you let me in? Let me be part of your life?"

Her lips hovered within a half-inch of his, and an answer came in the form of a kiss. He took her mouth hungrily, leading with his tongue and not stopping to let her follow. It seemed as though he meant to consume her, lips, body and soul. A powerful, primal kiss that Darcy fought to match in intensity but could not sustain. She felt herself drifting into submission, melting against him, relinquishing all control. Was this what it meant to be part of his life, part of him?

His hands squeezed her buttocks, grinding her against him, and her toes swung forward and back with the motion as her legs dangled freely on either side of him. She broke free of his kiss, wrapping her arms in a near stranglehold around him. She held her face against his unshaven jaw and nested her nose into the dark, curling masses of his hair. The scent of him drove her sensory receptors into orbit.

She would be spoiled for any other man for the rest of her life, and she knew it. But if the fates willed it, she would need no other. His hands left her rear, and glided up her back, then to her shoulders, pushing her apart from him to create breathing room. His nose rested on her bowed head, her forehead pressing into his chin.

"My life. Is. Complicated. You do yourself no favors if you enter it further."

Not the answer Darcy wanted to hear. He'd opened a door, but as good as forbade her to pass through it. She squeezed her eyes shut in denial. "You send the invitation, but don't want me to accept. Why am I here then?" She shook with the frustration of wanting him to continue, keep touching her, her hair, her breasts, every deepest part of her that he could reach.

Valor sighed deeply. "I'm out of line. I invited you here to help you with your experiments, and in turn your experiments may help me. Yes, we're a team in a sense, fighting this disease together. But this, this is wrong…you and me."

"Why? You didn't think so a moment ago, with your hands on my ass. What are you so afraid of? You don't look like the type of man…warlock…who could be afraid of anything."

He squeezed her shoulders so hard it hurt. Even then, Darcy could feel that he held back, that his true strength could crush her small bones into dust.

"I don't fear death, and I don't fear the pandemic of the Némesati. Only what it will do to our kind, our future. What I also fear is involving you in something so dark, so ancient, when you are so full of light and youth. I fear it will steal all of that from you, forever. And I can't bear that thought."

His words brought tears to her eyes. He cared for her, but perhaps not in the way she wanted. Protective yes, but condescending. Like she wasn't woman enough to understand him or his cause. Well, she would prove him wrong. It was her cause, too.

She pushed off him and stood with her back straight as though a steel rod ran through it, the scientist part of her coming to the fore. "Then let's solve this thing. Why are the samples so different?" she asked.

He looked at her with hooded eyes. "Because the virus mutates. It affects everyone differently, according to their DNA structure. The disease could literally have as many variations as it does victims."

"So, my mother's genes are predisposed to aging, and that's what the virus goes after?"

He nodded. "That's my postulation."

"So what do you make of the extraneous cell count in my grandmother's sample? What does it represent?"

"Probably a result of the mutation. The virus bonded with existing cells and spawned something new. It will be interesting to see the results of these latest cultures. What made you choose these three particular herbs?"

"I told you the symptoms. The yarrow and witch hazel act as anticoagulants; the bittersweet has neurotransmitter properties. I thought the combination of the three would slow the infection and promote brain activity at the same time."

Valor sat with his hands on his knees. She could practically hear the brilliant wheels turning in his handsome head. He was certainly a thinker, as well as a lover.

He looked up at her. "The Alternative Medicine conference starts this weekend, here in Boston. I think you should come with me."

Darcy blinked. "That's for MDs and Academicians, not wet-behind-the-ears undergrads like me. I'd be out of my league."

He rose from his seat and put his arms protectively around her, stroking her strawberry curls as they hung down her back. "You'll be with me. We're a team, remember? We're collaborating on a research mission. It only makes sense that we attend together. Unless you have other plans?"

She shook her head. "I can't think of any place I'd rather be, than working with you."

"Really? I get the feeling you can think of a few places," he said, flashing his eyes toward the bedroom.

"Bedroom work? Masters and Johnson would be proud." Darcy smirked.

Valor laughed, but quickly regained his serious disposition. "I should take you home, now. It's getting late."

Her good mood deteriorated. "Don't talk to me like I'm a child. What's with you? One minute you're coming on to me, and the next…"

"You are a child, compared to me. But you do have classes tomorrow, and if I don't get you out of here soon, you may not make roll call. And I would never forgive myself for that."

So the mighty warlock could be tempted, after all. "Oh all right, I'll go. But I'll be here right after class, to see the results!"

"Deal," he said, guiding her in the direction of the stairs. He slapped her backside in an attempt to get her moving. She spun around, shot him an indignant glare and put her hands on her hips.

"You're impossible. Maybe I'll slap you, next time." She continued toward the stairs, but stopped when something caught her eye. She picked up a small item from his office desk. "What's this?" She held Germayne's Horse Head token in her hand.

"Leave it there. It belongs to someone else."

Darcy fanned an impish grin. She chucked the little figurine up and down in her hand a couple of times. "I like it. Maybe I'll take it with me. To remember you by." He sent her a warning look, and she enjoyed his reaction. He seemed uncomfortable with her touching it. She jostled it from hand to hand, then stopped and closed one fist around it. The item seemed to buzz in her palm. Instinctively, she raised it to her nose and began to smell it.

Her nostrils twitched, and her eyes focused off in the distance the way they always did when she encountered a new *kathra*. She rotated the little chunk of metal, sniffing all sides of it. The tang of iron, like blood, made up the main component. An undertone smelled of earth, peaty and moist as if from a grave. The highlights, if they could be called that, stank of mold, of rotting mushrooms and other fungal growth. It smelled of evil.

Valor leaned against the lab counter and watched her intently throughout her performance, neither speaking nor moving. She dropped the figurine to the carpet. "Who does that belong to?" she asked, her face losing color.

He crossed his arms. "That, my dear. Is my problem, not yours. What were you doing? You look so pale."

She started to shiver. "I was...cataloguing."

"Cataloguing?"

"Yes. Now you know one of my dirty little secrets. I can record things, qualities, characteristics. Of an animal or a person. Or from an object that belongs to person, or that they've touched. Just by smell. I can't help it. And I can't forget it. It's permanent." She looked down at the little Horse Head. *This person is evil.*

She could hear Valor breathing in and out. "What happens when that person, or thing, comes around again?" he asked her.

"I'll know it. I sense it. It gets stronger the closer they are. It's like a warp signature, it's unique to them and only them. My mother called it '*kathra*.' She looked up at Valor. "I think she made that word up."

"No, she didn't. A *kathra* is exactly like that, a unique identifier, as you see it. But it's more than that. We use that term to describe a witch or warlock's soul. And you can smell them?" He looked somewhat incredulous at this notion.

"Yeah well, one of my little abnormalities. Don't tell anyone, okay?"

His mouth quirked downward. "My lips are sealed. Could you find this person, if you needed to?"

Darcy stuck out her bottom lip in thought. "I've never tried. But I suppose I could, if I was looking for them."

Oliviah, sleeping on the couch until now, leaped into Valor's arms. He smiled at the interruption and petted her between the ears. "Let's get the two of you home now." At these words, the cat dropped to the floor and ran to his office. Using the armchair as a springboard, she re-situated herself on top of the apothecary cabinet, out of everyone's reach. Her demeanour suggested she had no intention of leaving.

"I'll get her," he said, moving toward the cabinet.

"Oh, don't bother," Darcy scowled. "Pain in the ass cat. You can keep her for all I care."

Chapter Ten

When Darcy had left, Valor peeked into the guest bedroom to check on Shania. She'd been asleep the entire time he'd been in his lab with Darcy. And no wonder…the dose of morphine she'd begged for knocked her out like a title fighter. He raised the lighting with a flick of his index finger and went to her bedside. Her face had cleared again. Her hysterics over Germayne's alleged visitation brought a renewed fury at his treatment of Shania and the drug dependency he'd caused. He closed the door and went to his office.

If Darcy had Germayne's *kathra* in her little mind-catalogue, could she help find him? Lucie wasn't sure if Germayne was even still alive. Ironic that his demise would on one hand rid them of danger and on the other make the Némesati plague unstoppable.

He picked up the Horse Head charm from where Darcy had dropped it, and sat down in the armchair chair next to his desk from which Oliviah had vaulted herself. What did he have that Germayne needed so desperately? He could not forgive him for withholding his help when Artizia lay dying, and even worse, the unconscionable things he had done to Shania. Had he raped her? Held her in bondage? Made her succumb to his every depraved whim and fantasy with the promise of a drug fix? His stomach retched even to visualize any of it.

The Professor's book lay on his desk. He opened it now, making a mental note to register Darcy for the conference, and began to read.

*

Lucie ventured home after leaving McCaine's Pharmacy. Without knowing Germayne`s status she didn't see any point in hiding out and being uncomfortable. A nice flask of Dragonwine sat chilling in her kitchen, which she intended to enjoy in the comfort of a warm bubble bath. Her joints ached. Another symptom of the virus? Valor hadn't said so out loud, but she felt more and more certain she would eventually fall victim to this deadly scourge. If she could help Valor solve this biological riddle, would he finally come to her and be her love, not just her lover?

Being his consort would fulfill her. She'd give up her powers if needed, if it meant destroying the threat and becoming his wife. Yes, that had a nice ring to it…wife. She waved her arm across the antique, claw-footed bathtub and it filled with scented water and rich mounds of bubbles.

She admired her figure in the mirror as she stripped, removing her dress and letting it fall to the floor. Still pretty good for a woman of her age. She hefted her boobs with both hands as they protruded from the cups of her black satin bodyshaper and twisted side to side, observing their creamy roundness. She slid her hands down each side of her ribcage until they came to rest on her hips. Nice hips. She pirouetted to observe herself from behind. Ass still good, legs still killer.

Pulling the zipper, she slipped off the tight-fitting undergarment and dropped it to the bathroom floor. The bathwater soothed her tired feet as she stepped through the cloud of bubbles and sank into the fragrant warmth of the tub. She settled back and raised her palm into the air, summoning a goblet of Dragonwine. The bitter but rich green liquid relaxed her as it flowed down her throat. Sleep would come a little easier tonight, in a haze of Dragonwine.

She raised her other arm as though holding a conductor's baton, and music began to play. The sounds of classic jazz filtered throughout the room, upping the serenity level even further. *Perhaps things would turn out right after all*, she thought, with her perfect mini-universe tuned in all around her.

After a few more sips of Dragonwine, Lucie closed her eyes and hummed along with the melody of the current song. An old jazz standard, she began to punctuate her humming with the few lyrics she remembered, speaking them in an off-key whisper.

> *"Blue Skies, mm…mm...mm…mmm.*
> *Nothin' but Blue Skies…"*

Porter? No, Berlin, she recalled. The composer. She met him in New York after a performance there once, a lot of years ago. Irving Berlin had lived to see 100, but Lucie had been 100 long before that and she lived still. Unlike poor Irving.

> *"Never saw the sun…la la la la,*
> *Never saw things…la la la la.*
> *Noticing the days hurrying by,*
> *When you're in love, my, my, how they fly."*

The last two lines seemed to come without trying. Her memory must be improving. She opened her mouth to sing the chorus and realized an entirely different voice had joined hers. Her eyes shot open, and through a shimmering curtain of steam and Dragonwine after-effect, saw him. Sitting on the edge of her tub with legs crossed and hands interlaced over his knee, singing.

> *"Oh, Blue Skies, shining on me;*
> *Nothing but Blue Skies, do I see."*

The goblet of Dragonwine crashed to the floor and shattered on the cold tiles.

"Oh, are we in love, my dear old cousin? How sweet. You've dropped your drink. Let me get that for you," Germayne said in a saccharine voice. Sweeping his outstretched fingers, a new glass materialized in her hand. "Don't let me stop you. Continue please, your noble but sadly hopeless song of love for the doomed Doctor."

Lucie felt her lips go thick as sausages as she tried to speak. "I thought you…"

"Were dead?" he finished for her, his eyebrows raising a set of three furrows on his balding brow. "Did you enjoy spying on me? Did you learn anything at all?"

She kept quiet, her swollen lips preventing any sound from forming.

"Hmph," he snorted, disappointed with her silence. "I thought not. Well, let me educate you on a few things, then. Firstly, pine all you want for dear Doctor McCaine; he'll never be yours. Don't believe me? See for yourself the next time you drop by his place. Secondly, has that tingly sensation in your lips started yet? Nasty side effect of that Dragonwine…oh wait. Maybe it's the virus." He snapped his fingers. "Maybe it's the virus in your wine."

Lucie squirmed under her shield of bubbles, felt her body stiffening as if rigor mortis were setting in. *He's poisoned my wine, the freakbit!*

"Listen to me, Lu. He doesn't love you. He never will. You will only get sicker each moment you refuse me. Why do I know this? Why do I know you will suffer accelerated symptoms day after day, week after week?" He bent down nearer to her face and displayed another of his horrendous, saw-toothed smiles. "Because I created the virus. The Némesati, as our dear Hippocratic friend has labeled it. Such an elegant name for a horribly devastating condition. Robbing witchfolk of their powers to animate, apparate, conjure, curse or charm. Triggering every genetic propensity for illness, weakness, desire or abnormality. Can you think of a worse death? Dying from everything?"

Germayne actually cackled at this last statement, seeming to applaud his own mangled brilliance. Lucie lay helpless in the warm water. Her vision clouded, but her brain did not dim. She felt one tiny spark of satisfaction in that she'd been able to warn Valor, even though he did not seem to heed her words. What did Germayne expect her to see, at Valor's? Would he free her from this forced paralysis long enough to go to him? He must. For whatever reason, he couldn't get to Valor on his own and wanted her to set him up.

All these thoughts occurred to her in rapid sequence, but one outweighed all the others. She did not want to die. By creating the virus, he surely held the only cure, just as he said. Perhaps if she helped him, he would spare both her and Valor.

"Now then," Germayne continued. "Let's see about your condition. I can make it worse, or I can make it better. Let me show you."

Lucie felt her tight joints releasing, her muscles relaxing in blessed relief. A warmth flowed through her veins, surging to every pathway and capillary in her body. Then it began to sting, escalating until it felt like her very tissues were on fire. She raised her arms and legs, watching wild-eyed as her skin contorted into wrinkles and folds, and cysts formed beneath its surface, pushing painfully outward and preparing to burst. She screamed and thrashed about, her perfumed bathwater turning red and spewing over the edges of the tub, soaking the room.

Just as quickly, the pain subsided and her disfigured body returned to normal. The relief so great, she hadn't the strength to get up, get away from Germayne while she could. She lay prone against the smooth porcelain curves of her bathtub, legs and arms spread wide.

"Relax now," he soothed. "It gets better. So much better." He tilted his head, made a soft fist and placed it against the palm of his other hand.

A familiar twitch convulsed in Lucie's abdomen. Her back arched, and her breasts tingled. Heaven and Hell, no! She did not want to feel this way in his presence. A cool buzzing began in her inner thighs, spreading to her anus and then to her vulva. The areola on each breast tightened into rough brown disks, turning her nipples into throbbing spikes of flesh. Her pale skin, just moments ago tortured into diseased despair, now lay dappled in goosebumps, aroused from head to toe. Her crotch burned with the need for sexual release, her clitoris swelling and pressing her labia apart. Moist cream escaped from her vagina and coated her genitals in eager readiness for sex.

Her hands moved to stroke her alert breasts, rubbing the nipples and pinching their tips. She threw her head back, her unseeing eyeballs rolling upward. She reached between her legs, massaging herself from front to back, pausing to pump her middle finger in and out of her vagina several times, then swirling her juices around her pulsating clit. Her knees raised up and out, and both hands moved to her exposed genitals, rubbing and pumping, until she cried out.

She came harder than she'd ever come in her long, long, lifetime. Her moans echoed in the tall room, rattling the windowpanes. With a shrieking crack, the mirror above the sink split in two and slammed to the floor. Every bottle and jar flew from its place on ledges, shelves or cabinets and rocketed across the space to strike the walls in a cannon salvo of cosmetics.

Her orgasm lasted several minutes, unceasing waves of ecstasy rocking her body. When it stilled, Lucie collapsed in exhaustion in her now-empty bathtub. Water dripped from every wall and corner in the room, and Irving Berlin's orchestra still tinkled in the background. Her breath came in pants, gasping for oxygen as though her lungs had emptied of it. The best non-fuck she'd ever had…and couldn't wait to experience it again.

As she regained her senses, she realized Germayne had gone.

Chapter Eleven

The plenary session for the Alternative Medicine conference began at seven p.m. on Friday. With Darcy's classes running until four o'clock, Valor offered to meet her on campus and escort her to the convention centre from there. He'd already analyzed the test results, and unfortunately they posed more questions than they did answers.

His attendance at the conference did present another problem, what to do with Shania. He'd promised not to leave her alone, and while he thought of asking Lucie to keep watch over her, an unlikely volunteer stepped into the ring.

Ever since they'd met in Darcy's apartment, Valor and Oliviah had understood each other. The animal spoke to him in a wordless, ancient language he could not, nor would even try to explain to Darcy. It had been lost to history long ago, much as Gaelic or Sanskrit had among mortal languages today. He'd learned it through his medical studies, and then only through interest in the subject. He suspected Darcy had no concept of the cat's true age; likely much older even than himself. With sensory perceptions he could not even hope to acquire, and the fact she'd decided to make herself at home in his pharmacy, Oliviah made an ideal sentry.

Rain threatened from the cloudy skies overhead. Darcy stood under the awning of a Starbucks kiosk at the edge of campus as Valor's taxi pulled up. She looked like a woodland creature hiding from the impending rain, her cornflower-blue eyes luminous and pensive in the graying light. Her strawberry hair coiled into tight ringlets in the humid air. A short-skirted floral print dress exposed her shapely legs. Desire flamed in his experienced heart, despite his efforts to quell it and the wide gulf of years between them.

She waved and smiled, as he stepped onto the pavement to usher her into the waiting cab. Her freshness and lack of guile captivated him in a way he didn't expect and chose not to examine further. It felt good just as it was.

"Did the serum work?" she asked, excited. "Did it show anything different?" She huddled next to him in the dry warmth of the car.

"It showed promise. But not in the way you might have hoped." He slipped her backpack from her shoulder. "Do you have your tablet in here?'

"Yes," she said, digging it out from its padded sleeve.

Valor fitted a flash drive into its port to show her the imaging. "Sample one," he pointed at the screen. "Viral count down, but white cell count elevated." He swiped to the next image. "Sample two, extraneous cell mitosis abated, but viral count increasing." Swipe. "Sample three." He didn't comment, waiting for Darcy to form her own observation and/or conclusion.

"There's no growth." She touched her fingers to the screen and pinched the image smaller, larger, panned up, down, left and right. "The virus isn't even present. That's good, right?" She looked up at him with a half-smile.

"Depends. It tells us what it isn't, but not what it is. It's your blood sample, Darcy."

"I gathered that. But I shouldn't have the virus, anyway. I'm not a… a…"

"Careful," he interrupted, motioning to the cab driver. "It could be a number of causes. You might be too young to have had contact with the virus. Maybe you only have partial genetic susceptibility. You said yourself you're not sure what you are. You mentioned characteristics about your mother and grandmother. What about other family members?"

Darcy looked out the cab window. "If you mean my father, I can't say. I never knew a father. It's just been me, my mom, and my grandma for as long as I can remember." She returned her gaze to Valor. "And Oliviah."

"I'm sorry. I didn't mean to pry. I guess I am asking if your father was mortal."

Darcy shook her curly head. "I don't know. He wasn't discussed. If it's important, I could ask; if I told them it might help?"

Valor put his arm around her. "It can wait until after the conference. The important thing is your new formula did show results. You may be on the right track, just not the right plants. There's a session on naturopathic treatments tomorrow. I signed you up."

"That's thoughtful of you," she said with a tinge of sarcasm. "You won't be going to it?"

"I have other sessions in mind…we can cover more ground if we split up; gather more information. Agreed?"

She clucked her tongue. "I suppose."

They entered the convention center and found the registration desk. Darcy collected their badges while Valor signed them in and got their schedules. The token registrant gift was a laptop bag and matching notebook with the conference logo silkscreened on the front. Useful, but similar to a lot of other junk he already owned.

As they approached the speaker's hall, a distinguished gentleman perhaps all of five foot four with a wispy gray beard and wire-rimmed spectacles shuffled up to them.

"Sibelius!" Valor said, reaching out for a handshake. "Wasn't sure I'd catch up with you until tomorrow."

"Tomorrow waits for no man, McCaine. Glad to see you could make it." Professor Sibelius grinned and pumped Valor's hand vigorously.

"Isn't that: 'Time waits for no man?'" Darcy interjected.

Sibelius regarded her from behind his progressive lenses, tilting his line of sight to put her in focus. "Why, yes, so it is. Just my little twist on things, my dear. Altan Sibelius, at your service," he said, offering her a similar, hearty handshake. "And your name is…?"

"Professor, I'd like you to meet the author of that whitepaper you gave me. Miss Darcy deHavalend," Valor said.

Sibelius' eyes seemed to widen. "Are you, now? Fascinating paper! How is it we haven't met, Miss deHavalend? I've been around this campus so long, I didn't think anyone escaped my notice."

"Perhaps it's because you only teach the 300 and 400 level subjects, Professor," Darcy answered. "I'm only in second year."

"Ah well, it won't be long before I'll see you in my classes. I'll bet you're ready for the 300 lectures now, judging by the content of that research."

Darcy smiled. "You flatter me, Professor. I'll look forward to it." She turned to Valor. "I'll go grab us some seats, okay? While you and the Professor finish your conversation," she said with a wink.

Valor nodded, noting her attempt to break away from

Sibelius. He couldn't help watching her shapely buns sashay from side to side, swinging the hem of her short skirt as she disappeared into the crowd entering the hall. He also noted that the Professor couldn't help it, either.

Sibelius put a fist to his mouth and coughed to clear his throat. "Little young for you, don't you think, McCaine?"

One side of Valor's mouth curled into a sardonic grin. "You've no idea, Altan."

"So let's see your schedule there, what sessions are you in for?" the Professor asked, changing the subject.

"Oh, this and that," Valor answered, handing him his printed schedule. The Professor looked it over, lifting his nose to view through the lower part of his lenses.

"Ah, yes. The Nootropics session will be of interest. Attending that one myself," Sibelius said, handing the paper back. "Find anything useful in that volume I gave you?"

"Oh yes. Remind me to return it to you."

The Professor waved his hand in dismissal. "Keep it. I think you need it more than I ever will. Hope you find what you're looking for."

"Thanks, Altan. Shall we?" Valor indicated the entrance to the speaker's hall.

"Lead on, dear boy."

*

When the opening ceremonies finished, the conference centre lobby filled with attendees streaming out from the speaker's hall. Darcy and Valor wormed their way through the milling bodies toward the guest bar and the exits.

"I could use a drink," he commented as they neared the bar. "How about you?"

Darcy twisted to face him. "After two hours of scientific monotone, yeah. I sure could." They both laughed and edged their way to the bar, Valor ordering a Scotch and Darcy a beer.

"Your poison of choice?" he asked, as the bartender poured the drinks.

"Of course. Student, remember? Beer budget."

"It's on me."

She wagged a finger at him. "Don't get me off track. Beer today, gone tomorrow."

"Whatever you say." Valor smiled as he watched her heft her beerglass and take a hearty swallow. He started to realize that the more time he spent with her, the more he enjoyed it. So unlike anyone in his ancient circle of acquaintances. As much as his work and the present danger made him feel his two hundred years, this girl, no…woman, he admitted… made those years peel back. He found himself actually looking forward to the future. Something he hadn't felt in quite some time.

"What?" she asked from behind the rim of her glass, noting him staring at her. A tiny ring of foam coated her upper lip. She wiped it off with a cocktail napkin. "Okay, not very ladylike, I get it. But I'm thirsty."

He shook his head. "That's not what I was thinking."

Her cornflower blues seemed to expand as she returned his stare. "Oh? Just what are you thinking then, Dr. Masters?"

"Not now, Dr. Johnson. I was just thinking about…the future. Your future. You have a bright one ahead, I'm certain of it."

She swirled the remaining beer around in her glass before taking another sip. "You make that sound like you won't be around to see it," she said warily.

He shrugged. "You never know; I could be the next fatality."

Darcy swiveled her head to throw him a questioning,

sideways glance. Then her brow knotted in thought. "We never took a sample of your blood. Does that mean you've already tested yourself?" His continued silence brought on a look of alarm to her freckled face. "Val…er…Valor…"

"Val is fine." He liked the sound of it, coming from her luscious lips.

"Val," she repeated. "Are you holding back? Is there something you're not telling me? God, all this time, I never gave any thought to whether you might be sick…" Her voice broke off, her eyes flitting upward to the ceiling as if admiring the light fixtures. Her nostrils flared, her gaze again taking on that distant look he'd observed in his office. He watched in fascination as she sniffed, tilted her head, sniffed again. Her blue eyes took on a leaden hue.

"That person…is here," she whispered.

Valor stiffened, glancing from side to side. That answered the question of whether Germayne were alive or dead. "Where? Close by, or…"

Every light in the center went out, plunging the crowded room into utter blackness. Waves of voices moaning "ohhh" and various profanities washed over the space. Bodies jostled them as people moved about in confusion.

"Val," he heard Darcy cry, and sensed her being pushed to the ground. He reached out and caught her arm, raised her up and pulled her close.

"Are you okay?" The emergency lighting kicked in and they were able to move toward the exits. A woman screamed, and all eyes turned to her. A commotion began around her, people backing away, some stooping toward the floor.

Tittering voices ensued. "Someone's collapsed," they heard, and "Is he all right? What's wrong with him? Call an ambulance!" Valor started to move in that direction, but Darcy's tugs and the press of so many people held him back.

"Hey," she said. "The place is swarming with doctors, let's just go, please…"

Against his instincts, he acquiesced and ushered her out of the building. Even if Darcy had 'smelled' him, it wasn't the right time to face Germayne, in a crowd like this.

*

"What is it you want me to do?" Lucie asked in a flat voice, devoid of emotion. They stood in the same alley behind the coffee shop they'd visited just days before, where Germayne had made his initial threats.

"I need to get inside his pharmacy, his laboratory. Lead me there, and I'll do the rest."

"Why do you need me? Can't you just apparate inside the shop?" Lucie's nerve and resolve wore thin. "GerMayne, the All-Powerful?" She kidded him, not in jest but in acerbic sarcasm.

Germayne narrowed his yellow eyes. "In case you haven't noticed, Doctor Dreamy has significant powers and resources, even if he chooses to use them in weak, altruistic ways. His home is guarded by the *Entrada Neos* charm, in addition to several layers of…force field, let's call it. Electromagnetically tuned against certain DNA signatures."

Lucie smiled inwardly. Trust Valor to combine 'craft with sophisticated science. One of the plethora of things she loved about him, his brilliant mind. To think she might be the agent of his safety gave her a triumphant little thrill. Nothing could make her betray him.

"What will you do once you're in?"

Her cousin lifted his chin in condescension. "Are you going to help me or not? You've seen the consequences of 'not.' Do not tire me further, Jezebel. You will regret it."

"I can't help you unless you tell me your entire plan. Wouldn't want me screwing up, now would you?"

"No." Germayne licked his thin lips. It reminded Lucie of a rattlesnake flicking its forked tongue out in warning. His expression softened, and tilted his head as he considered her, analyzing, calculating. "Tell me, did you enjoy your…spa experience the other night?"

Lucie did enjoy it, but felt repulsed at the idea of even recalling the memory of it in his presence. Even the voice he used to ask the question made her skin crawl. But she wanted more, no doubt about it. The most intense sexual encounter ever, and it had brought her kinetic powers raging to life. She felt stronger for it.

"Yes," she answered in a small voice. "Will that be my reward for helping you? I hope you don't have to… participate…in order for me to collect."

Germayne actually laughed at this, throwing his head back and guffawing with his hideous dental work on full display. "Trust me, cousin. I've no compulsion for incest, and to be truthful, I don't find you that attractive. You will have the power to invoke that satisfaction at any time or place, with or without anyone present. In addition, all traces and residual effects of the virus will be eradicated from your body. Isn't that worth sacrificing one feckless warlock's soul, to save your own?"

Lucie ground her teeth in irritation. *Keep your cool, make him trust you. Find out everything you can.* "How do I know you'll keep your word? What happens if something goes wrong, even if I do what you ask? I want that power, Germayne, win or lose."

He looked at her coldly. In an instant, Lucie felt her insides twist and buckle, as though a live animal had lodged there. Sweat beaded on her forehead and chest, and her breath came short. Her hair felt as if it too, came alive, its curling strands standing on end and writhing about her scalp like tiny serpents.

"No negotiating!" he shouted, but only in her mind. His rough, baleful voice shattered her eardrums from within. "Or I'll kill you now, if you prefer."

Lucie raised her hands to her clammy throat, saw her delicate skin turning green. Then she vomited, incapacitating retches following one after another, spewing black mucous and pieces of animal flesh onto the garbage-filled pavement. When the convulsions eased and the last bits of bile dripped from her mouth, he spoke aloud.

"Go to him. See what company he keeps when you're not around. Then I will tell you the plan."

The warlock disapparated. Lucie remained conscious only long enough to see her skin return to normal and her puddle of vomit vanishing before she blacked out cold.

Chapter Twelve

"I want to check the samples myself." Darcy said, from the dark comfort of the taxi as it sped away from the city's center.

"It's late," Valor said. "You should go straight home, get some rest. Long day of sessions tomorrow."

She snuggled next to him in the rear seat, her head fitting into the crook of his armpit. She toyed with the buttons on his jacket. "I know, but I'm serious. I want to try a different ratio of the herbs and run the test again. Right now, tonight."

"Why tonight? It can wait. I need you sharp for the conference."

She twisted to look him in the eye. "I can be sharp right now. If you want me to." Her invitation dangled suggestively in the air. "Besides. We have to be at the same place at the same time tomorrow. Why not just leave from your place? Save you an extra cab fare," she argued.

"Are you asking to spend the night with me, Dr. Johnson? In the name of science?"

Darcy smiled. "Of course, Dr. Masters. We are collaborating on research, are we not?"

His violet eyes twinkled in the sweeping, intermittent light from the street lamps as the cab cruised along. "And I suppose you miss Oliviah, too," he said, deflecting the implications of her comment.

"Oh, terribly. May I see her, please?"

"All right," he said. "But after you tell me more about... what you smelled."

She settled back against him, gazing forward out the front windshield. "I hope that man's okay. The smell kinda stopped after he fell down, or whatever."

"Go on," Valor prompted.

"Sometimes it does that, it disconnects if some sudden or traumatic event occurs." She thought about it some more before speaking again. "I got a sense that the 'presence' made a mistake. Wasn't supposed to be there, or changed its mind. Something." She shrugged. "I'm glad though. That *kathra* is not a nice person."

"Anything else?"

After a moment, Darcy shook her head. She couldn't put into words the unbalanced, dizzy feeling the evil *kathra* projected upon her. It's what made her fall. Better to say nothing until she figured it out. She didn't want to get drawn into a long discussion that might kill the romantic buzz she felt growing between them. The cab slowed at it reached McCaine's pharmacy, but continued another half block before turning into the alley behind the row of shops. It stopped at the rear entrance to McCaine's.

"Back door man, huh?" Darcy joked.

"Safer this way. Come on." Valor exited the cab and held his hand out to assist her. She clasped his hand willingly, and stepped onto the cobbled surface of the back lane. The taxi drove off, and he guided her to the back entrance, where the motion sensor light flipped on at their approach. He waved a hand at the deadbolt mechanism. The lock released and the door swung open.

"That's a neat trick. Wish I could do that."

"You can get one at any hardware store," Valor deadpanned, meaning the sensor. Darcy swatted him on his sleeve. The interior lights came on, revealing a storage area for deliveries and a staircase leading to the second floor. Valor paused, then took her by the hand and led her up the steps. Darcy's heart rate elevated, reveling in the warmth of his grasp and the promise of what intimate moments might follow. She'd long since abandoned any trepidations about their difference in age, or her forward behavior. It felt right being around him — exciting, electrifying. Science was the last thing on her mind.

They reached the upper floor, and true to form, Oliviah launched herself at the two of them as soon as they opened the door. Valor caught her as she landed against his chest, and lifted her to sit on his shoulder. Darcy felt a tad nervous at what 'conversation' might be occurring between the two, now that she knew Oliviah could communicate with the doctor.

Valor set the cat down on the armchair by his desk. Darcy stroked the length of her from the top of her head to the tip of her tail, grasping it in her hand like a rope. "What have you been up to this evening?" she asked.

"Oh, you know. Sleeping. Stretching. Eating. Busy night."

"Don't get too comfortable here, Missy. You live with me, remember?"

"Right. And why are you here, at this late hour? I know how you think. We won't be going home anytime soon."

Darcy yanked Oliviah's tail, eliciting an indignant yowl.

"Hey! That's no way to treat your familiar," Valor scolded, offering to take Darcy's coat.

"Familiar?" Darcy retorted. "I've no such thing. This

furry bag of bones is just…the family curse. I'm stuck with her. Or you are, if you're not careful."

Valor chuckled, hanging her coat on a rack near the door. "I don't mind. I told you, I like cats." He turned to face her. "So. All the materials are over there. What did you have in mind about the proportions of the herbal extracts?" He gestured to the lab area.

Darcy looked at him helplessly. "You bought that?"

He stepped toward her, crossing his arms. "Not really. But I'm giving you the benefit of the doubt."

"I think altering the ratios would be a logical step." Darcy said. "But I also think we need to add your blood sample to the test." She looked at him seriously, then strode over to the lab. "Roll up your sleeve?"

Valor raised an eyebrow. "Do you know what you're doing?"

"I watched you. It's not that complicated. Unless you'd prefer to do it yourself?"

He unfolded his arms and moved to the lab, sitting down obediently on one of the stools. "I have had a drink, you understand. Go ahead." He watched as Darcy retrieved the hypodermics from a cabinet. He extended his arm and she repeated all his steps, attaching the rubber tourniquet and dabbing the puncture site clean with an alcohol-soaked cotton puff. She grasped his forearm, and jabbed the needle into his exposed vein like an expert. The plastic vial filled with his blood.

Neither spoke, then Darcy looked up into his eyes. He met her gaze in an even, calm manner, telegraphing a deep sense of trust and surrender. It seemed right. In a few moments, she released the tourniquet and withdrew the needle. She applied pressure with the cotton ball and taped it to his skin. "There. Wasn't so bad, huh?"

"You'd have made a good nurse," he said, bending his elbow to stop the blood flow. "Now what?"

"We make the serum," she said. "Where are your culture dishes?"

Valor pointed to a cabinet behind her. She turned and rifled through the cabinet, while he went to the fridge for the herbal extracts. In a few minutes, they had all four blood samples readied and placed them in the incubator. Darcy had increased the proportion of yarrow and bittersweet for this test.

"Well, that's that," she said. "Now all we have to do is wait." She turned a watery, blue-eyed look his way. "What are we going to do until first session tomorrow?"

Valor returned her provocative stare. "I don't know. What is it you would like to do?" Darcy thought she might melt like the Wicked Witch of the West under that heated glare. She crossed slowly to where he stood.

"Valor McCaine. I realize we've not known each other long. And that there's a significant age difference between us. But I want you to make love to me. Take me now, please. Here, in your home, in your bed."

He stood only inches from her, yet seemed to hold her at arm's length. She held her breath, laying everything on the line, waiting for his response. All or nothing, now. The suspense seemed interminable.

His expression turned hard, looking her over as one might appraise a hip of beef. Before she knew it, he took her fast in his arms. "Darcy. Please do not mistake my hesitation for disinterest. I am only thinking of your own welfare. There will be no coming back if I comply with your request. Are you certain this is what you want? Say now, because in a few moments, it will be too late."

She shuddered for the want of him, and the realization of what he meant. No commitment seemed too great to be possessed by him, even if only for one night. "I want this," she said. "With all my heart. Take me now."

He lifted her in off her feet and carried her to his bedroom. He laid her forcefully on his bed, an antique four-poster with mile-high comforters piled upon it. He grasped at the front of her dress, popping the buttons quickly and slipping the top of the garment off her shoulders. He shoved one bra cup aside and sucked her breast with abandon, taking the whole of her nipple into his mouth, grazing it with his teeth, biting down then licking the soreness away.

Darcy panted like an animal, arching her back to present her tits to him in any way he wanted. She clawed at his shirt, finding the buttons with shaking hands and twisting them open. He raised up, straddling her and holding her to the bed with his powerful thighs, then wrenched the shirt from his torso and cast it to the floor. He hoisted up the hem of her skirt, exposing her lace panties. His fingers slid inside the waistband and forced them down below her buttocks.

He paused, a gentle sigh escaping his lips as he looked over her half-naked form, tits out and pussy bared. "You are so incredibly beautiful. I don't deserve to take you this way."

Darcy had no words to respond. Her crotch throbbed, waiting for his touch. She reached for the clasp on the front of her bra, released it with a quick twist and let her breasts tumble out, unfettered.

He reached for them, fondling them in slow circles, rubbing his thumbs over her stiff nipples, wringing exquisite pain mixed with pleasure. Her hands went to his belt, releasing the buckle and fumbling for the zipper. He caught hold of her hands, pushed them away and eased himself back to the edge of the bed. He slipped off his pants and underwear and dropped them to the floor. His excellent body lay in full view above her, a smooth chest with tight brown nipples, defined abs and sculptured pecs. The most beautiful specimen of a man she'd ever seen.

Her eyes went to his fully aroused cock, rippled with veins and stressing the limits of the skin that covered it. He leaned forward and removed her panties, drawing them down the silky length of her legs and over her toes. They landed on the floor with the rest of Valor's clothing. He prowled onto the bed, arching over her with one arm on each side of her legs. Then he leaned down, pushed her skirt up higher and pressed her knees outward, exposing her pussy wide before him.

Darcy trembled all over and held her arms to her chest, fisting her hands to stem the quivering. No man had seen her this way, ever, and she wasn't sure what to expect. His hands slid down the skin of her inner thighs toward her center, and when he lowered his head to her crotch, thought she might die of shock and pleasure as his tongue reached out to touch her clitoris.

She let out a painful gasp, the act so new and erotic to her, her brain could barely process the sensations. Her back arched instinctively, her hips wanting to buck, but his powerful hands held her thighs down and apart. She was at the mercy of his seeking tongue. It lapped at her clit, then dove into the cleft of skin between her clitoris and labia, first one side then the other. Then it returned to center, wiggling her tender nub side to side.

The building pressure toward orgasm made Darcy moan aloud with each breath. She'd never known such pleasure and her head spun in confusion and ecstasy, indescribable colors and patterns passing before her eyes.

"Not just yet, sweet Darcy," she heard his voice whisper, his head withdrawing from between her legs. His lips kissed the soft skin of her thighs, left then right, working his way back to her knees. "But soon, when I am inside you."

He brought his body overtop her, his muscular chest rubbing against her bare breasts, and his thick cock pressing against her soaking wet pussy. He nuzzled her throat and placed tender kisses along her jaw and chin. He lifted his face to hers, their lips nearly touching.

"Taste how sweet you are," he breathed, then kissed her in that same hungry way he'd done while standing in his office. His tongue thrust into her mouth, letting her sample the flavors he'd collected from her aching pussy.

Darcy smelled and tasted her own juices, a heady blend of salt and starch and musk, the idea utterly foreign to her but powerfully erotic at the same time. She brought her hands to his face, fingers splaying across his jaw, holding him to her and drinking in the sensory kiss.

He reached down and guided his penis, slippery with the mixture of her cream and his own fluids, into her waiting vagina. She felt the light pressure of him entering her, then the rush of full penetration, more wonderful than she ever imagined. At last, they were truly together. They broke their kiss, Darcy's hands leaving his face to glide around his neck and rest on the taut muscles of his back. His first thrusts were strong and slow, his cock so large it bumped her cervix each time. This made her cry out, not in pain but in sheer intensity of feeling.

"Darcy," he said, his breath accelerating. "I don't want to hurt you, tell me to stop if you need to." He continued to pound into her, each stroke faster than the last.

"No," she whispered, knowing her voice shook with emotion. "Don't stop, don't stop…you won't break me." She felt near crying with joy, having this man make love to her. She realized then, as he'd said, there would be no going back.

Darcy raised her knees and wrapped her legs around his waist. His groin slapped against her as his rhythm increased, pushing to the hilt as he neared climax. In this position, her clit received a healthy bump with each stroke, and it finished her. She wailed in uncontrolled abandon, quaking rushes of orgasm wracking her body. Her nails dug into the skin of his back, as he made his final plunges into her before he too, came.

Suddenly, Valor's voice ripped through the space, sounding more like a cry of pain than of pleasure. Then Darcy realized that not only her own claws tore at his skin, but Oliviah's too. The animal landed on them like a furry missile.

Chapter Thirteen

Oliviah's voice shrieked inside Valor's head. *"Didn't you hear me? Your somnaeturnum spell wore off! Shania's awake and coming this way!"*

The tremors of his ejaculation still rocketed his body. Perhaps the cat had been trying to warn him even earlier but he couldn't hear her through the cloud of emotions during sex. He didn't expect this...the spell should have kept Shania under for hours.

He rolled away from Darcy, their bodies moist with perspiration. Oliviah skittered off the bed and leapt to a position of safety on top of a wardrobe. He grabbed the edge of the tousled comforter and covered Darcy as he looked toward the bedroom door.

"Hey," she squawked, confusion in her voice. In the rectangle of light from the open door stood an unclothed, disheveled Shania. She leaned one bent arm against the doorframe, one leg poised to step further into the room. Her head tilted sideways, observing the scene as though she did not understand. Unkempt blond hair framed her face in strawlike wisps and dangled down past her shoulders, brushing her naked breasts. She stood there like a nightmarish Lady Godiva, eyes dilated from heavy doses of drugs.

Darcy squealed and clutched the fabric of the comforter to her chest. Vaoor's heart ached at seeing her expression, looking as though she wanted to hide, run or die; anything but sit trapped in his bedroom with him and some crazy witch.

"Darcy, I'm so sorry," he said, holding out his hand like a stop sign. This isn't what it appears. Just stay calm, I can explain." He turned to Shania. "Shania, go back to your room and go to sleep. This doesn't concern you."

Shania's wild eyes took on a dark glow, and instead of doing as he asked, took a tentative step toward the bed. She seemed fascinated with Darcy, looking her up and down. An impish smile formed on her plump lips, and her hands began to caress her own breasts.

"Did you bring us a playmate, Valor? That's brilliant, why didn't I think of that?" She edged nearer to the bed, and Darcy recoiled, scooting backwards into the headboard. "Does she like to fuck?"

"Get her out of here!" Darcy screamed.

Valor jumped off the bed and made a move for Shania, grabbing her by the wrist and twisting it behind her back, forcing her to face the doorway. He scooped her up and carried her bodily out into the hall and back to her bedroom. She squirmed and kicked her feet, but could not wriggle free of him. He deposited her onto her bed without ceremony.

Shania giggled. He guessed she must have helped herself to more morphine or other drug she fancied in his absence. She looked bedraggled and high as a kite.

She sat upright on the bed. "You have a nice cock. Did you fuck her with it? Why won't you fuck me with it?"

"Be quiet," he scolded. "You're sick, you need rest. Lie

down, cover up, and I'll bring you something to make you sleep."

"You said you wouldn't leave me alone again." Her giddiness faded into pouting resentment. "You're a liar."

Enough. Valor trained his eye on her, held up one hand, then lowered it slowly to his side. As he did so, Shania's eyes closed and she lay back upon the bed, commanded back to sleep by his spell. He covered her and raced back to his own bedroom, loathe to even think what Darcy would be feeling at this point.

As he reached the doorway, he nearly bumped into Darcy as she tried to exit, fully dressed and clutching both Oliviah and her sling bag in her arms. "I'm leaving," she said, her voice and gaze as cold as ice. Valor felt more naked than naked. He felt exposed in every way, physically, emotionally and morally.

"I said I would explain. You know better than to jump to conclusions, Darcy deHavalend, BSc. Don't leave…let me get dressed and we'll talk." He reached for his clothes that lay heaped at the foot of the bed.

"What can you possibly explain?" she asked with fury. "There's a sex-crazed, diseased girl living with you. Maybe more than one, for all I know. Maybe it's a hobby, or… jeez, maybe some kind of experiment, like the Island of Dr. Moreau. Was I next on the docket?"

She was screaming now. Valor could accept she had every right to scream. "You watch too many movies," he said, donning his pants and shirt. "Listen to me. Her name is Shania and she's my patient. She's a victim of this same virus, and her life is in danger. I offered to keep her here — she's my best friend's daughter. He died several years ago."

Darcy quieted down, but continued to glare at him.

"She also has a drug problem. You saw her state of mind, she's sick. She's been abused. She needs my help." Silence hung between them for several moments. "And I need your forgiveness. Please don't go."

Darcy looked at him, hot tears welling up and threatening to overflow onto her cheeks. "This is too weird. I...I...can't even..." she broke off, choking on the words. "I have to get out of here." She turned and ran for the back exit, her shoes clattering down the steps.

Valor let her go, even though a simple spell could have kept her in the room if he'd wanted to. He would not impose his will on her; her free spirit had attracted him from the beginning and he wasn't about to crush it now. Perhaps Oliviah would talk some sense into her. He straightened the bed and sat down on it, pondering a million things going through his head. What to do with Shania, what next steps to take with the tests, track down the not-dead Germayne and end this senseless duel between them.

He crossed to his office to pour himself another Scotch, knowing he wouldn't sleep a wink anyway. There above the overstuffed armchair, floated Lucie. She levitated in midair, a sickly glow emanating from around her body. If looks could kill, the expression she wore would have smote him dead a hundred times over. Her pupils flared red like laser pointers and her fingers curved into raptor-like claws, ready to strike. Even her hair seemed to come alive, writhing like Medusa's, black and silver serpents intertwining and caressing each other.

"You." Her voice croaked in an unnatural octave that dripped with hatred. "Are a faithless, immoral blackguard. You deserve to die."

He circled around her in slow, measured steps. "Lu," he said evenly. "What's going on, why are you here? Are you sick? Do you need help? Let me help you."

She hissed at him like a feral feline. "Help me? You cannot help me. Betrayer! Casanova!" Her laser eyes sparked like roman candles. "You carve my heart just as you carve your patients with a knife! Look at you and your…coven of concubines. I was a fool not to see the depths of your depravity. Yes I am sick, because you make me sick!"

Valor shook his head, unwilling to believe these words came from Lucie herself. How long had she been in his home, watching, listening? Staying invisible until now. She must be under some influence. Had Germayne caught up with her, found her spying on him? He'd known her so long…this wasn't her. More than ever he wanted to save her. He spoke in a soothing, gentle tone.

"Lucie, darling. You know that I love you, you're dearer to me than family. Please let me help you." He moved closer, readying a relaxation spell in his mind to cast upon her and immobilize her. Her eyes followed him like the crosshairs of a trained weapon. Just a few inches until he could touch her.

"*Go to hell!*" she screamed, and disapparated. His fingers closed around lingering yellow smoke.

*

Darcy stumbled across the lane outside McCaine's Pharmacy, sobbing miserably. She tripped over one shoe that had come loose in her haste to leave Valor's bedroom. Oliviah flopped from her arms and yowled in indignance as she hit the ground.

"Ouch! Watch what you're doing! You should listen to what the man has to say…you're being childish!"

"What would you know about it?" she snapped back. A lone taxicab pulled around the corner and slowed to a stop in front of them. Did the man have every taxi line in the city at his disposal? "Leave me alone. We're going home."

*

She knew he'd be waiting. He reclined on the park bench, one knee bent with his foot resting on the seat and the other dangling to the ground. As sunrise neared, the horizon behind him awakened in gentle tones of yellow and orange. Lucie felt tired beyond all measure, drained and disheartened. What Germayne had told her held true. Valor didn't care for her. In the end he only told her those sweet lines to save his own skin. She'd watched the entire time, the drug-addled blond lying in his guest bed, masturbating and fantasizing about him while she waited for his return. Then he arrived with that curly-headed infant, barely old enough to menstruate, on his arm. To top it off he had the gall to fuck the girl, too. The poor thing had no concept of who or what Valor really was.

And now, Lucie knew too. A womanizing, lascivious bastard who used his patients for his own sexual gratification. He didn't matter in the grand scheme of things. She stepped up to the park bench, her words escaping as puffs of vapor in the chill dawn air.

"Cousin. Tell me the plan."

Germayne smiled, his cruel features turning almost pleasant with the knowledge she'd come onside. "Dear, dear Lucie," he said, holding out his hand for her. She grasped it, her own cold fingers drawing warmth from his. "You see things as they really are, now. There, there. Don't fret. It's for the best. Just think of how strong and powerful and— satisfied— you'll be when we're rid of him and the rest of those who refuse to join us. Better times are ahead, trust me."

He pulled her to sit next to him on the cold bench. Better times seemed far away, with her heart in pieces and feeling as if all life had been sucked from her veins. "I believe you. What do you want me to do?"

Chapter Fourteen

Saturday dawned with the ache of regret pounding in Darcy's head. She awoke with her pillow bunched into her face and her fists clenched beneath it. Awful scenes that had replayed in her nightmares revealed themselves as truth in the cold light of day. Though she'd only had one beer, her guts churned as if ten tequila shots rioted inside them.

She shifted beneath the covers, noting a warm, weighted lump nestled close to her backside. She reached out and stroked its furry exterior and the lump began to purr. This ranked as atypical, the animal normally preferring her own bed inside the Rubbermaid tub. But Darcy took this as a sign of support. Despite her cantankerous attitude, Oliviah would be true to her for as long as she lived. This small comfort made daylight bearable.

Darcy slipped from the bed and padded to the bathroom. She groaned at the frightful reflection that greeted her in the mirror. Her eyes rimmed in red from crying, shocks of reddish curls standing to attention in ten crazy angles— hideous! Having hit the bed in an anguished heap last night, her unwashed face now sported several pimples, too. Did life get any worse? In disgust, she wrenched the shower taps on and shucked her bra and panties to the floor before stepping into the downpour of hot water.

She was no virgin, but sex with Valor McCaine might as well have been her first time. She'd been so sure, so infatuated with him, she'd cast all caution to the wind, not even insisting on a condom, for God's sake. She'd lost her head, plain and simple. The vision of that frightful girl standing in the doorway made her shudder. *Patient, my ass.* How many girls had he kept in his 'office' over the years? One too many, in her opinion. She refused to be next.

She finished her shower and dried off. She had to move on, remember her purpose. The conference sessions began in a few hours, and she was determined to make the most of them. After she'd dressed and made toast, she picked up her cell phone and dialed her mother.

"Hello, dear! How are your classes going?" Her mom's voice sounded weak and throaty. "Good, mom. I'm going to a conference today, a major one that only doctors and professors usually get to attend. I think I'll learn a lot. How are you doing? How's the weather in Phoenix?"

"Oh, I'm fine, we're fine. Still hot and dry. Grandma had a bit of a relapse yesterday, but nothing we can't cope with."

"A relapse? Like what?"

"It's nothing, nothing for you to worry about. Had a bit of a meltdown is all. She's frustrated, of course. Her roses are dying, and she's not able to walk much at all with the pain in her joints. But we're managing."

Darcy's heart clenched, wishing she could be with them instead of stuck in her bachelor flat a thousand miles away. "That's good. Anything I can bring you, when I'm on semester break?"

"Just yourself. We've got a big thanksgiving dinner

planned…all the relatives will be here. They all want to hear about your college life."

Darcy chuckled, but it raised a painful question. "It's not that exciting, really. But it will be nice to see everybody. Mom…"

"Yes, dear?"

"I know we never talk about this, but something's come up and I need to know. Was my father…normal? I mean, did he have your kind of talents?"

Silence hung over the cell waves. "Oh, Darcy. I'm sorry to have kept anything from you all these years. It just seemed safer, keeping him out of the picture. You haven't suffered for it, have you? Your grandma and me, we took care of you, didn't we?"

"Yes, of course. I don't feel like I missed out on anything. I was just curious. I'm working on a…genealogy project," she said. It wasn't exactly a lie. "Heredity, recessive and dominant traits, that kind of stuff. If I don't have the same skills as you and grandma, I got to thinking maybe my father was probably a regular guy? I'm sorry it didn't work out between the two of you. Don't think for a moment I've ever felt unloved, or disadvantaged. It's not my business, I just wanted to know."

Her mother heaved a long sigh. "He doesn't know about you, sweetheart. I had to keep you a secret, for your own safety."

"I understand. I love you, Mom. What do you mean, for my own safety?"

"Your father was a powerful man. Too powerful. His ego got the best of him and he wanted nothing to do with settling down or living a family life. As to why you didn't inherit his 'skills'…" She broke into a fit of coughing. Darcy listened with sadness to the painful, wretching spasms. "I'm not sure," she continued, after recovering. "But it's a good thing, really. Having too much of anything, even power, is dangerous. I'm glad; you're perfect the way you are."

"Guess I won't argue that point," Darcy said, her voice light. "Was he handsome?"

Her mother laughed. "Oh, my word, yes. And charming, and arrogant, self-absorbed and a hundred other things. I quite lost my head over him, as I'm sure plenty of others did after me. I regret it now."

Lost her head? Darcy winced inwardly. Hadn't she just said that about herself? About another powerful, charming, handsome Warlock? Regret didn't begin to describe it. "Can you tell me his name?" she asked.

"If it helps you, yes. His name was, and still is, I assume, Germayne Aucoin."

*

Valor scrubbed Shania with an astringent elixir made from Yarrow and Witch Hazel. She leaned forward obediently in the bathtub full of bubbles as he did so. The red lesions had spread to her shoulders and back, and sitting in bathwater seemed the only time she could remain calm and lucid. He chalked up her atrocious behavior of last night to the unpredictable reaction of the infection with random amphetamines she'd found in his apothecary cabinet.

He had noticed one thing, however. The drug combination had alleviated her anxiety and feelings of paranoia. Her skin also seemed to clear during these episodes, as they also did when she was sexually aroused. Could endorphins play a part in slowing the spread of infection? At any rate, he'd not been helping her much. Keeping her under lock and key certainly wasn't the answer. How awful that must have looked to Darcy. No matter how honorable his intentions, he would have difficulty explaining Shania's appearance.

"Feeling better?" he asked her, rinsing her skin with the warm water from the tub.

"Mmm-hmm," she murmured. "Where did you go last night?"

"I went to a conference," he said.

"Oh. I was asleep. When did you get home?"

Valor blinked. Did she not remember her actions from the night before? "About eleven. Didn't you hear me come in?"

"Nope."

He wished Darcy would have the same lack of memory. He didn't expect her to show up at the conference today, and he didn't blame her. But the test samples in his lab might hold some information she wanted. He took this thought a step further.

"Shania. Towel off and get dressed. I want to take a blood sample from you, if that's all right?"

She turned toward him with a shy smile. "Anything for you, Valor."

*

An hour later, Valor made his way to the conference centre armed with new information. Unlike yesterday, the sun shone overhead and illuminated the turning leaves of the trees that lined the boulevards and parks of Boston. He hurried to his first session, Nootropics and their effect on Brain Tachometry. He remembered Sibelius saying he would be attending, and he had a few questions for the Professor.

The speaker's hall filled with eager conference-goers, and Valor barely got inside. As he signed the attendance form, a friendly voice called to him. "McCaine, how've you been, man?"

He looked up to see an old colleague, Rutger Sheldrake, smiling and reaching for a handshake. "Rutger," he said.

"Just fine, and you?" The two men shook hands and moved off toward the rows of folding chairs in the auditorium.

"Oh, a few years older and deeper in debt," Sheldrake answered. "Situation normal. Shame about Altan, though, hey?"

"Altan Sibelius? What do you mean? He's supposed to be here today, have you seen him?"

Rutger shook his head. "They took him away in an ambulance last night. Collapsed right there in the foyer," he said, gesturing out the doors. "He's at the University Hospital now, haven't heard how he's doing."

Valor hid his rising anxiety. "That's too bad. I'll have to check in on him after sessions."

"Yeah, me too. Catch you later." Sheldrake went to join a few others on the other side of the hall. He cursed himself for not getting through the crowd last night, knowing now it had been Altan that had fallen ill. It seemed unconnected, but the coincidence of Germayne's presence, according to Darcy, and Sibelius' collapse gave him pause.

The speaker took the lectern, and the auditorium lights dimmed. He found a seat and prepared to absorb any new insights he might find. After a windy preamble, the presenter launched into the meat of his topic.

"These substances are being used as neuroenhancers, collectively referred to as 'smart drugs.' The most popular are methylphenidate, or MPH, and dl-amphetamine. You know the former as Ritalin, an ADHD medication, and the latter as Adderall, or its more pal-sy name of "Addy". Sounds like something your aunt would give you, doesn't it?" A titter of laughter washed over the audience. The speaker droned on.

"Both drugs increase a class of neurotransmitters called monoamines. These neurotransmitters, dopamine, serotonin and norepinephrine – as you know, control mental functions like motivation, attention, pleasure, alertness. Preferentially increasing these neurotransmitters in the prefrontal cortex activates certain circuits while suppressing others; like a radio, they increase the signal-to-noise ratio of neurotransmission, allowing improved focus on the task at hand."

Valor listened intently. Sibelius had intimated certain things about psychotropic drugs when they'd talked; no wonder he'd been keen to attend this session. Would neuroenhancers combined with plant-based stimulants possibly super-boost telekinectivity?

"…Surveys indicate students in pharmacy and medicine – where memory work is key – use stimulants to improve academic performance and potentially boost learning in a lecture setting. On the negative side, excessive use has also led to Stevens–Johnson Syndrome or SJS, and Toxic Epidermal Necrolysis, TEN, two forms of a life-threatening skin condition…"

This part caught his attention…necrotic skin conditions. Like Shania, and what Darcy had described about her mother's rapid aging.

The remainder of the lecture touched on other pharmaceuticals in common circulation, surgeons using a wakefulness-promoting drug called Modafinil, then segued into naturally-derived psychedelic substances such as Psilocybin and Harmaline. The latter, extracted from the South American Banisteriopsis Caapi vine, was said to promote not only psychokinetic experiences and abilities but enhance sexual performance as well.

At the conclusion of the presentation, Valor knew he had to find two people. Darcy, and Professor Sibelius. He'd chosen all of Darcy's sessions himself, so if she turned up, he knew where to look. He hurried to the next forum on her schedule.

Attendees exiting the adjoining hall made scanning the crowd difficult, but with his heightened visual acuity, spotted Darcy in a back corner, earbuds in and tablet on her lap. She clearly appeared to be shutting herself off from the world around her. But she was here. He admired that, and felt an irrational twinge of pride that this young woman could overcome her emotional state and choose to be proactive about her vocation. He approached her cautiously. "Darcy."

She not so much heard him as sensed him, when she looked up from her notes. She sat silent, waiting for him to make the first move.

"I'm glad you're here. I'm sorry for last night," he began. Her mouth twitched, and she removed her earbuds.

"Sorry. Couldn't hear you. What did you say?"

Valor sighed, and took the empty seat next to her. "I said, I'm sorry for last night. And I'm happy to see you here. Did you sleep well?"

"What do you think?" She stared at him, unblinking.

He pulled the flash drive from his pocket. "I thought you might want to see the results of our latest test."

She took the flash drive from him and plugged it into her tablet. He waited while she swiped through the images at her own pace, hoping she'd find the same significance in them that he did.

"This is good…this is…really good." She looked up with the beginnings of a smile on her freckled face. "The viral growth has slowed in every case. Even the extraneous growth has tapered off. These last two are perfect. No sign of infection at all. One of them is mine?"

He nodded. "And the other is mine. We both appear to be immune, or at least resistant, to the virus. We could potentially develop a serum. Are you game to try again, Dr. Johnson?"

Darcy's weak grin faded. "Please don't make fun. I made

a mistake in trying to be close to you. It won't happen again. If you mean try again on a professional level, then maybe. I have as much at stake in this as you do."

"Agreed." He had no wish to hurt her further, even though she didn't fully appreciate the complexity of his situation. "I've just come from a very interesting session that I'd like your input on."

Her chin dipped as she shot him a wide-eyed glance, and pointed to herself. "Moi? Input?"

"Yes. We're still a team aren't we?" He didn't wait for a response. "Have you, or any of your fellow students used Ritalin or Adderall, to help them study or pass an exam?"

Her mouth set in a firm line as she considered his question, then nodded. "Yes. I haven't personally, but I've heard of kids who do. Not a fan. That's why I work with herbals."

"Ironically, the active substances in most of the plant phenols are the very same that the drug companies harvest, propagate, refine and sell to market as supplements. I'm thinking if we use a combination of these along with the herbal compounds, we may find a way to combat the degenerative mental conditions as well as the virus. What do you say?"

"It's worth a try."

Valor smiled. "Good. I'm going to track down some of the drugs. And Darcy..." He reached out to touch her arm. "I am truly sorry about last night. I told you the truth. It's up to you whether to believe me or not. You didn't make a mistake. But perhaps I did. In falling for you when I'm old enough to know better." He stood to leave, taking a good long look at her before turning away. He'd only taken a few steps when she grabbed him by the sleeve.

"Val," she said. He stopped in his tracks. "Where are you going?"

"To see a friend. You remember meeting Professor Sibelius yesterday?"

"Yes."

"Well, unfortunately he's the man who collapsed in the crowd last night. He's in the University hospital, and I'm going to check up on him.

"Oh, no. May I come with you? He seemed like such a nice man."

"Are you sure you won't get too close to me?" He held out his hand.

Darcy looked at his open palm, then slipped her hand into it. "I'll take my chances."

Chapter Fifteen

Altan Sibelius lay in a partial upright position in his hospital bed, gazing out the window and sipping water through a bendie straw.

"Hi."

The professor turned his head. "Well, hello McCaine. Good of you to come. Hope you took notes." His voice rasped in a painful way.

Valor chuckled. "Yes sir I did. But frankly, you've more important things on your plate right now than the conference. Like getting well. How are you feeling?"

Sibelius waved his hand meekly. "Frustrated more than anything. Damn nuisance being laid up like this."

"I've brought a friend," Valor said, leading Darcy into the room.

"Hello, Professor."

Sibelius' expression lit up like a lamp. "Why hello…oh, this is better than medicine and sunshine put together! A visit from an up-and-coming science major, and a pretty one, too. Come in my dear, so kind of you to stop by."

"My pleasure, Professor. I hope you're feeling better."

"What happened last night, Altan?" Valor asked. "Sheldrake told me you collapsed at the conference."

The professor drew in a long breath and exhaled in a wheezing cough. "Damndest thing," he said. "One minute I was chatting with my cronies, and the next everything went black."

"Literally," Valor remarked. "The power grid blew and the whole conference centre went out. We left after that."

Sibelius looked curious. "Really? How odd."

"I'm sure it was due to your electric personality, Professor." Darcy teased.

He waved a finger at her. "Don't you be flirting with me young lady," he said with a smile. "Once I'm out of here, I might give my learned friend here a run for his money."

"You may have a coronary just entertaining that thought," Valor said. "Or I might switch your lights off permanently, if you try muscling in on my girl like that." They all chuckled. "What else do you remember?"

The Professor held up his empty water cup with the bendie straw. "Would you mind, dear?" He looked at Darcy.

"Of course not," she replied, taking his cup and refilling it from the sink in the bathroom.

Altan crooked his index finger at McCaine. Valor leaned in closer. "This is for your ears only, understand?" Valor nodded. The professor's eyes took on a mysterious cast, and inhaled a harsh breath. "Do you believe in witchcraft?"

Valor blinked. It wasn't the first time in his long life that he'd been asked this question. His answer usually depended on who did the asking. In this case, he said the following:

"What I believe is of no consequence. What matters is that there are those who do."

Sibelius gave a tiny, knowing nod. "Well, I didn't before, but I do now. During my blackout, I had what I can only describe as a visitation. Evil. Powerful. Invasive. It took something from me and left me powerless to stop it. Horrible, ghastly feeling."

Valor listened with dread. "What did he…it…take from you?" *Oops.* He didn't mean to lead Sibelius to any preconceived notions.

"He?" the professor queried, pursing his lips in thought. "I wasn't thinking about gender, but now that you mention it. 'He' seems appropriate. He took the most valuable thing I have left. Knowledge. And left me something in its place." He convulsed in a spasm of coughing. Darcy returned with the water and held the cup and straw to his lips. When he'd settled down, he took several sips.

"Death. He left me death. Check my chart, McCaine. You'll see the bloodwork."

"Altan, don't talk like that. You know how the mind works, you're going to be fine."

"It doesn't matter. The knowledge was taken from me, from my mind, by force. A force beyond natural science. You have to gain the same knowledge, McCaine, to fight this."

Valor glanced at Darcy, judging her reaction as to how much and what she'd heard, then returned to the professor. "How? What am I fighting?"

Sibelius lifted his hand and began tapping Valor's chest repeatedly. "Go to my office. There's a hard drive in my cabinet, a red one. Get it." His hand uncurled to reveal a set of keys on a small ring.

Valor took them from him. "All right. I'll be back to see you later. You call me if you need anything, yes? Or if these nurses aren't treating you right," he whispered with a wink.

The professor nodded, and collapsed into another coughing fit. "Shall I press the call button?" Darcy asked, reaching for the remote unit that lay on the bed. Her forehead wrinkled in concern.

"Do it," Valor said. He grabbed the chart from its holder

at the foot of the diagnostic bed, but had a sinking feeling he already knew what it would reveal. Germayne had finally done the unthinkable, and broken the most sacred code of them all. He had given the Némesati to humans.

*

They left the hospital, Valor preparing to go to Sibelius' office while Darcy returned to the conference. "Find out whatever you can from your sessions. I'll go get the professor's records. Will you meet me at my office afterward, to go over all the findings? I'll cook dinner, if you'll stay. I promise we won't be interrupted."

Darcy's head swam with a million contradictions. Stay. Go. Trust, don't trust. Keep your guard up. Cut him loose. Forgive him. Which to go with? Her heart never felt wrenched in so many directions. Above it all lay a simple truth she could not deny. She wanted to be with Valor. The word dropped from her lips before she realized it. "Yes."

He smiled the same one-sided smile she'd fallen in love with the first day in his pharmacy. In an unexpected move, he scooped her into his arms. His lips bent near to her ear. "Thank you," he whispered. "For your trust in me." Then he released her, his hand lingering on her face, cupping her jaw in his palm. "See you at six."

Darcy watched him walk away, the street traffic swallowing him up until he disappeared from view. By this time she knew that all the taxis, all the walking, were just a front to blend in with mortalkind. Valor McCaine could zap himself anywhere on Earth at any time. He could also disappear from her life just that quickly if he chose. But he chose not. This gave her hope. She turned and walked back to the conference centre, determined to learn all she could to help the man she now realized she loved.

The conference wrapped up near four o'clock. Darcy

rubbed her eyes after a long afternoon of staring at projector screens, listening to speakers with foreign accents and taking copious notes on her tablet. She had time to run home, pick up Oliviah and head back to McCaine's Pharmacy. She took another look at the slide imaging Valor had brought her this morning. The test results were very encouraging. With the addition of 'smart drugs,' maybe they could beat this thing after all.

When she unlocked the door to her apartment, she braced herself for the usual bullet of fur to shoot out into the hallway and race to her perch on the newel post. She stuck her foot into the opening to try, just once, to foil the cat's plans. Oddly, no calico-coated body even met her at the door, much less bolted from it.

Darcy frowned, and peeked into the room, half expecting her saucy companion to be playing a joke on her and hiding around the corner to leap on her in ambush. "Oliviah?" she called. The room seemed far too still. As she stepped inside, an aura of uneasiness took hold. She set down her sling bag on the old couch and went straight to the Rubbermaid tub in the kitchen, hoping to find her sleeping there. The makeshift cat bed lay empty.

"Oliviah?" she called again, circling the room. A faint, pathetic meow sounded from her bedroom, and she raced for it. There on her bed, the poor animal lay prostrate, her limbs stretched out and her lithe body hunched in pain. "Oh my God," Darcy shrieked, running to her. Oliviya's golden eyes shone round as full moons, her pupil slits contracted to mere slivers. Saliva dripped from her open mouth as she panted, her belly pulsing up and down with each rapid breath.

"Help me..."

Darcy wrapped the bedsheet around the quaking Oliviah, and lifted her into a mesh hamper she kept in the bathroom. With sturdy carry handles, it resembled a market basket more than a laundry receptacle. For now, it would do as a pet cargo container. She hauled the basket to the door, picking up her sling bag as she went, and left the apartment without bothering to lock up. He may not be a veterinarian, but Valor McCaine was the only doctor she would trust Oliviah to. A Witch Doctor.

"Please don't die, please don't die." She repeated this mantra over and over in the cab ride across town. She held the mesh basket on her lap, rocking it back and forth. "Oh, hang on, Oliviah, hang on. I'm sorry for all the mean things I said. Please don't die, I need you." The cabbie must think her mad, talking to a lumpy bundle of cotton sheets, but she didn't care. Weak, pitiful yowls sounded periodically from the basket. The fact that no further words had come from her beloved animal troubled her even more. Perhaps she was beyond saving already.

Darcy pushed this thought from her mind as they reached McCaine's. The neon sign in front glowed CLOSED as dusk drew in. It wasn't six o'clock yet. Valor must have closed the shop for the day to attend the conference. "Can you pull around back, please?' she asked the driver. Rounding the block seemed to take forever in her distress over Oliviah, but at last the vehicle pulled up to the pharmacy's rear entrance.

The motion-sensor flicked on as she reached the door. She hadn't thought about whether to knock, ring the bell or just go right in, so she did all three. The deadbolt was unlatched, and the door swung open with a twist of the knob. He had been expecting her, after all. She lugged the basket up the stairs and into the office.

"Val," she called. "Help. Oliviah's sick!" The room lay dark and quiet. "Val?" She lifted Oliviah from the basket and began to unwrap her on Valor' desk. The poor thing twitched miserably, the fur on her face wet with saliva and her tail curled about her legs. A piteous half-grunt, half-howl escaped from her throat. Darcy filled a petrie dish with water and brought it to Oliviah's mouth. "Drink, Missy. Please."

Oliviah's ear flicked, and her parched tongue lolled out to lap a few drops of water. Darcy stroked her swollen belly. "Val?" she called again. "Where are you?"

"In here," she heard his voice. "Come here, you have to see this."

Valor's voice sounded strained, not his usual smooth baritone. She covered Oliviah with part of the blanket and followed the sound. She went past the examining area, saw one of the bedroom doors open and the lights on. "Val, what is it? Please have a look at Oliviah, I...I think she's dying!"

She crossed to the open door. There, on the bed, lay the crazy girl from last night. Her hands and feet were bound, her eyes wild with fear. Her lips quivered as though she wanted to speak. Her short, frightened grunts clearly begged for Darcy to come nearer. *What the hell?* No, after all he'd told her, could her Dreamboat Doctor McCaine actually be into this? BDSM and such? Her heart shook with nausea and fear.

The look on the girl's face...she struggled to remember her name...Shayna? She seemed too terrified to be a willing participant. Darcy took a step closer.

The door banged shut, and Darcy whirled about, scared out of her skin. The black-haired apparition stood, no, floated there, her image seeming to swell and grow as she glared at Darcy with her teeth bared. She cackled with laughter befitting a sorceress. Stringy, black and gray ringlets framed the beyond-pale face, perforated by garish lips painted in a color so red...

She'd seen this woman before. Out on the front street the first night she'd arrived by taxi with her lab gear in tow. Dear God, another player in Valor's sick, sadomasochistic little entourage? Fear, betrayal and sickness overwhelmed her, and she sunk to the floor.

"That's it, just go to sleep, baby-bitch," Darcy heard, spoken in Valor's voice that yet was not his voice. Sparks flared in front of her eyes, then fizzled as darkness swallowed her.

Chapter Sixteen

The information on Professor Sibelius' hard drive had consumed Valor's entire afternoon, making him unable to return to the conference. Years of documentation, spelled out in minute detail, offered both everything Valor had hoped to find, and nothing he expected to find.

Since the 1960's, the *au courant* professor had experimented with psychotropic drugs. Not on himself necessarily, though his writings clearly showed he was not above taking a hit or a toke on a semi-regular basis. His original directive seemed bent on expanding the mind, unlocking the untapped potential of the human brain. As a result, he'd compiled a veritable compendium of drugs and their psychokinetic properties. The professor held a fortunate position of respect among students, colleagues and contemporaries who literally lined up to help him in his research.

This allowed Valor to narrow down what he should try. One of the keys he held in his hand unlocked a stores cabinet where all of the aforementioned substances could be found. Bittersweet had been only a minor find in

Sibelius' formidable drugstore, and a considerable amount of information on herbal compounds with psychotropic properties also existed in his reports with the same level of detail.

Later on, Sibelius' research focus swerved to disease and genetics. It became clear the professor had identified the Némesati, though not entirely understanding where it had come from nor naming it, as Valor had.

Where would the man have gotten samples of the virus? Until now, it had only affected his kind. It seemed illogical that the professor knew any witches or warlocks, particularly with his statement that he didn't believe in witchcraft until his unfortunate incident of yesterday. But then, how would the professor really know who was a witch or a warlock in this day and age? It's not like they walked around with ID cards.

Valor read on, delving into the reams of clinical data combined with actual lab experiments. Many of them mirrored Valor's procedures, and he appreciated the irony of how much he and the professor might have accomplished together if they'd known they were working toward the same goal. At the end of the clinical trials, Sibelius had compiled a list of formulas.

He'd numbered them all, hundreds of them, recipes for serums derived from all of his work and the sources of his materials and suppliers. Repeated entries referred to a shipping company, Pandora Imports, as the resource for most of his bio-hazardous goods as well as controlled substances. The naming convention appeared to be a date, a letter of the Greek alphabet and a serial number. However, the last entry on the list bore a different style of name.

Valor clicked on it, expanding the entry into more detail. This appeared to be the crowning glory, the wonder-drug Altan had claimed did not exist. *Sanguis Prima.* First Blood?

As he read through the data, things became clear. All the drugs and plant phenols had to combine with blood antigens to form the working serum. His interest in Darcy's report made complete sense in that light. The serum, *Sanguis Prima*, had stopped the virus cold. The evidence lay before him in black and white.

He had no doubt now about what 'knowledge' Germayne had stolen. Without sole ownership of the cure, Germayne had no power to wield over others and rendered his 'revolution' moot. Valor memorized the formula letter by letter, numeral by numeral, rather than making a copy. He checked the professor's stores for a preparation of *Sanguis Prima* but even if it were there, he realized it would be stupid for the scientist to label it as such. However, there were plentiful supplies of chemicals: Ritalin, Adderall, Psylocilbin, Serotonin, and many more.

So, that left Valor to make his own batch. In standard pharmaceutical practice, a serum would be derived from injecting a low-level, innocuous form of a disease into a host to produce antibodies. Whose 'First Blood' carried the benign form of the disease that Sibelius used to create the antigens, and where would he have obtained it? So far, the only people who showed immunity were himself and Darcy. The answer came to him as a spear through his heart. The reason Germayne held the only cure to the affliction was because he carried it. He'd refused to help eradicate it because he himself had created it, spread it, all for his own purpose. Further, he had to eliminate anyone who might discover the cure. That meant three people. Altan, himself, and Darcy.

Darcy! He'd asked her to meet him at six. He'd lost track of time. An old-fashioned grandfather clock occupied a corner of Sibelius' office, and it read nearly seven p.m. He returned the hard drive to the cabinet and locked the exit door from the inside. He had no need to leave the room that way.

In the next instant, he materialized in his own office. The lights were out, the place empty and unusually cold. Had the power gone out and stopped the furnace from igniting? A whimpering noise drew his attention to the strange lump that lay on top of his desk. Where was Darcy? He approached the desk, the squirming ball of fabric reminding him of an abandoned infant. He half expected to find a note attached.

He lifted the blanket away and saw Oliviah's broken form within. The animal lived, but just barely. In their shared ancient tongue, Valor asked her, *"Who did this to you?"*

"I do not know. I have met death many times, my friend... do not worry. I am not important for now. You have to find Darcy and Shania. They've been taken."

"Taken? What do you mean?"

"Look around....see for yourself."

Shania's empty bed and the condition of the room illustrated she'd not gone willingly. Clothing and blankets lay strewn everywhere, the nightstand upended and its contents spilled. One end of the curtain rod hung loose from the wall at an angle, the draperies pulled down where she'd clung to them. Lain over the pillow were two articles of clothing. Shania's silk nightshirt, and Darcy's jean jacket. On top of these lay the Horse Head game token, and a note tied to it with red ribbon. "Touch me," it read. Valor picked it up, and Germayne's message appeared inside his brain on contact. The game piece was now a holojector—an inanimate object imprinted with a visual signal transmitted via the body's natural electrical conductivity.

Images of Darcy and Shania, terrified and held against their will, projected into his mind. Their fear permeated the transmission, clawing at his heart, the message simple: *give yourself up or they will both die.*

He released the token, and his broad shoulders sagged
in exhaustion and surrender. Enough games. The time had
come to end this. With a slashing motion across his throat, he
rescinded the *Entrada Neos* spell and returned to his office to
tend to Oliviah. As he leaned over her forlorn little body, he
switched off a device next to his computer that resembled an
ordinary external hard drive. The power light blinked out and
stopped transmitting the specialized EMF wave that had kept
Germayne at bay. *Let the bastard come,* he thought.

He stroked Oliviah's matted coat, bristled with dried
saliva and fluid that leaked from her ears. *"Are you in pain"?*
he asked.

"Do not concern yourself. Pain is transitory."

He admired the animal's strength and wisdom. He wanted
to do something, ease her suffering at least. *"I'm going to
take some of your blood,"* he said.

"Do what you feel you need to."

He readied a syringe, and extracted just enough of
Oliviah's blood to examine under a microscope. In a few
minutes, he confirmed the presence of distemper and several
other common feline infections, all piled up on one another.
Very strange, and stranger still the suddenness with which
the diseases had attacked. Knowing that the Némesati
typically amplified the victim's latent ailments, he took a
guess that the virus had spread to witchkind's familiars as
well, and worked the same way.

The cat's vitals were plummeting. He made a decision,
and injected the remaining serum that he and Darcy had
prepared the previous evening into the thick skin around her
neck.

"Thank you honey," were the last words Valor heard from
her.

*

The sick atmosphere cloyed at her. She wanted to scratch it away from her face and throat. It tightened like a spiderweb, gruesome and sticky and stubbornly clinging to her skin. Even breathing seemed more difficult beneath this unseen mask of darkness and humid air. It smelled of earth, of mold, and rusting metal. She could not free herself of it, even if her hands were untied.

Darcy crouched on her knees in this dark space, her fear mounting but trying to hold on to a sense of the rational, the sane, the analytical. She remembered the red-lipped sorceress, trapping her in the bedroom with the sick girl… she still couldn't form her name with any certainty. After that, they'd been transported here, the trip unclear, just bits of images and sensations returning to mind. Like being shoved through a black hole, her body and mind twisted and stretched and propelled into space. To the dank of this place.

She could hear the other girl nearby, shifting her feet, wheezing and moaning frequently. She thought of poor Oliviah, lying helpless in Valor's office. Perhaps he was there now, tending to her. Would he have any idea where to look for her? Could Oliviah tell him anything—if she'd even lived long enough for Valor to reach her? This thought made her eyes sting. Crying would not solve anything…and she couldn't even wipe the tears away with her hands bound behind her. Until she knew otherwise, she chose to believe the cat would live…and Valor would come to find her and…

The frustration of not remembering the girl's name made her angry. Though sickened by the idea she might have been part of some creepy ménage, the girl lay trapped here just like herself. Darcy shifted position to more or less face in her direction.

"Hey," she whispered. "Can you hear me?" A moan. "I said, can you hear me? What's your name?"

Dry lips smacked against one another as the girl formed a speaking voice. "Shania."

"I'm Darcy. Any idea where we are?"

"We're in the time-out room," Shania said without hesitation.

Well. That said something…Shania had obviously been here before. Time-out? Time out from what? "Where's that, are we still in Boston?"

Shania's wheezy breathing shortened, and transformed into a helpless snicker. "Still…in Boston." Snicker. "Did you say your name was Dorothy? No, we're not in Boston anymore." Her giggling escalated into fearful laughter. "That's funny. Not in Boston anymore, Dorothy."

"Darcy," she corrected. "What's a time-out room? Have you been here before?"

Shania calmed down. "This is where he sends me when I don't behave." Darcy could hear her moving, laying down on the dirt surface beneath them. "You know. Time-out."

This did not sound promising nor helpful. "So. We get out then, after what? Counting to 100? Writing lines? Apologizing to someone? Who is "he?"

"I don't want to talk about him. I hope he lets me die down here."

"We're not going to die. If someone wanted us dead, I think we'd be that already. Come on, how do we get let out?"

Shania started whimpering. "When you behave. I'd rather die. Maybe you will, too."

The girl was nuts…wanting to just lay down and die. This was going nowhere. Darcy wriggled her hands, testing the bonds. They didn't feel like chain or cord or rubber tubing. They didn't feel like anything really; she just couldn't break her hands free.

"Hey, can you move your hands?" she asked Shania.

"Sure. Can't you?"

"No, they're tied."

Shania crawled to her, feeling her way to Darcy's hands by way of her feet, legs, thighs, elbows. Unlike herself, Shania seemed free as a bird. She recoiled a bit from her clammy touch. Shania grasped her wrists and uttered one word.

"Libre."

Darcy's hands separated instantly. Okay…Witch. She got it. Shania belonged to Valor's kind, not just some drug-addled prostitute in his care. So why couldn't Shania just zap them out of this dungeon?

"You're a witch?" she ventured.

"Aren't you?" she returned, after a silence.

"No. Can't you uh…use your powers to escape?"

Shania sat close to Darcy, their thighs touching. "This place is like a combat bunker. Shielded by his spells. Don't you think I'd have tried to get out before?"

Logical. Darcy changed tack. "Who is 'he'?"

"The most powerful warlock there is. And the most dangerous."

Shania brought her face close to Darcy's, her breath floating sweetly under her nostrils. Her *kathra* bloomed fierce and heady in Darcy's olfactory receptors. Moss and roses, thick red wine and patchouli. Primal, needy, wanton.

"He'll want to have sex with us," Shania whispered. "But we won't enjoy it." Her tongue darted out and licked Darcy's cheek. A hand stroked her arm, glided downward to clasp her freed hand in hers. "Better to take some enjoyment now. Being out there with him is the same as being dead, anyway."

Darcy shuddered at this sudden, unexpected sexual gesture. She tried to exhale the hypnotizing *kathra* from her sinuses, but the invasive nature of it lingered, sending its beckoning tentacles up to her brain. "You're crazy. Get off me, are you a lesbian?" In the dark, in tight quarters, she had no room to move away. Shania kept hold of her hand, and cupped Darcy's breast with the other. She gave it a squeeze.

"I'm just me…" she said, nuzzling Darcy's ear. "Why don't you just be you?"

Shania's hand slipped inside Darcy's blouse, beneath her bra cup and stroked the skin of her breast for real. While horrified, Darcy still felt both nipples peak hard at the girl's touch. Shania's tongue coiled into Darcy's ear, licking and circling. The sensation so foreign, so intimate, Darcy's reserve began to crack, her aversion falling away like plaster chips.

So dark, so hot. No one around to see, hear or care. Not even herself. Her tits ached.

Shania's mouth moved across her cheek, and kissed her full on the lips.

She had no idea a woman's kiss could be so good. Sweet and strong, sensitive but confident. Even Valor's kisses were not like this. She found herself going with it…a wicked thrill spreading from her chest down through her belly, making her limbs tingle and her pussy moist.

Shania's lips left hers, but added a quick smack for good measure. "You see? You can just be yourself around me." She grabbed Darcy's hands and placed them on her own breasts. "Why don't you try it?" With their hands doubled on top of each other, Shania massaged her breasts, forcing Darcy to feel them along with her. She shifted their weight back and forth between her hands. Darcy could feel their smooth and supple texture, her thumbs rubbing against the hardening pebbles of her nipples.

Darcy's brain reeled with conflicting urges. To stop and get as far away from this creature as possible, and at the same time move closer, explore farther, touch and be touched. The latter tantalized her, called to the hidden demons within her, coaxing her to stay.

"Suck them," Shania said, placing a hand behind Darcy's neck and pulling her head toward her bosom. "Go on." Her cheek pressed against the roundness of Shania's breast. It felt soft and good. Darcy's tongue ventured out and teased the nipple, licking the wrinkly areola in a circular path. Shania giggled as her nipples went harder. "Let me do you now."

Shania pushed Darcy back against the rough surface that formed a wall of the enclosure they were trapped in. Her fingers undid the buttons on Darcy's blouse and the clasp on her bra. In a flash, she had a breast in her mouth, slathering it with saliva and sucking deep and hard.

In the utter dark and suffocating warmth, Darcy's mind let go, conscious only of the mind-blowing sensations rocketing through her body. "Fuck…" she gasped. "Fuck that feels good."

Chapter Seventeen

"How long do you think it will take for him to come here?" Lucie asked, pacing the wooden floor. Germayne had turned an abandoned warehouse near the harbor into a sort of operations base for himself. The interior now resembled an eighteenth century drawing room with paneled walls, period furnishings and its tall, narrow windows covered in billowing yards of velvety drapes. He relaxed in a wing-backed chair, drinking liberally from various bottles of vintage liquor he'd procured.

"Oh, he's not coming here, Lu."

She spun on her pointed heels and stared at him. Her nerves were ragged as it was, without all this procrastinating and his cryptic comments. "I thought that was the point of kidnapping those two little tarts! What do you mean he's not coming?"

"We're going to go to him," he said, polishing off a brandy. "Frankly my dear, it won't do just to kill him. We have to kill his business, too. Destroy his tools, his practice, and his home. So that even his memory will be…" he paused and smiled. "…Gone with the Wind?"

He laughed at what Lucie assumed he thought to be a

clever, ironic turn of phrase. She rolled her eyes. "When? Why are we standing around?"

Germayne set his whisky glass down with a bang. "When he turns off all that techno-crap surrounding his office. And he will. He's far too soft-minded to leave our two little beauties to suffer. He can feel their pain…you left the holojector, correct?"

She shot him a look that said, 'don't ask such stupid questions.' She continued pacing. "And when he's dead? What of our two 'beauties,' then?"

"Well, that's up to you. Kill them if you like. Or perhaps you might think of something more interesting."

Lucie's head swiveled toward him, one dark eyebrow arched.

"I have a feeling your newfound libido would get an even bigger jumpstart if you put those two to good use." Germayne waved his hand to produce a holographic projection that hovered in midair. Lucie watched, her red lips parted in a lustful gape as she observed the scene playing out within the projection. Her crotch felt hot as she saw Shania sucking on Darcy's tits like a hungry calf. She held Darcy's fingers to her own cunt, rubbing herself into a frenzy. The two writhed upon the dirt floor of the time-out room in a private little orgy made for two. The liquor bottles rattled on the tabletop as Lucie's arousal mounted.

"Enough," she said. At the snap of Germayne's fingers the picture folded into oblivion. She refused to let him turn her into as jaded and debauched a creature as himself. She preferred to hang on to what few morals she had left, after committing kidnapping…and soon…murder. "Let's get going and kill the bastard."

*

Valor watched the animal's life signs fade. He'd done

all he could, but the feline unfortunately did not respond to the herbal-based serum, and he felt stumped as to why. Worse, he'd grown fond of Oliviah. After two centuries of witnessing all manner of loss and death, the suffering of an animal still moved him to tears.

He stroked her coat mechanically, staying with her until her lungs moved no more. Then he wrapped her body in clean sheets and returned her to the mesh basket, which he placed in a cool storage unit — a meat locker, for lack of a better descriptor. When he got Darcy back, as he swore he would, he would have to break the news of Oliviah's death gently.

He had no clear idea of where Germayne might be holding the two women. The holojector carried images and audio, but no GPS reference points. He could only wait for the inevitable. He might as well make good use of the time and get to work on Sibelius' *Sanguis Prima* serum, and perhaps devise a trap for his old contemporary.

In less than an hour Valor had several vials of the serum ready, using his own and Darcy's blood cells for the bio components. He still hadn't formed a complete hypothesis on Darcy's immunity. Without knowing her complete genetic history, the serum based on her blood might be risky at best. He wouldn't know until the latest cultures had developed which might take another twelve hours or more.

He turned his attention to the most pressing problem… where to find Germayne and therefore Darcy and Shania. With his personal shielding disconnected, it would only be a matter of time until Germayne turned up. Valor had to be ready.

He brought his mind back to a time when they considered themselves compatriots, colleagues; if not equals, at least soldiers of a common cause. Germayne, the elder of the two, assumed a sort of mentorship role with Valor. He chided himself when recalling he may have actually admired the man at one point. Germayne had seemingly limitless knowledge and effortless command of his 'craft. Oh, how he'd wanted to be like him in so many ways.

What had divided them? Valor thought on this, and realized that a turning point had always been Valor's decision to become a doctor. When he no longer sought power for the sake of power, this set the rudder of his life's voyage on a different trajectory from Germayne's. Shortly after, he'd met Artizia and thought, at the time, he had life by the balls and could want for nothing more.

Until the Némesati pandemic struck.

Considering these memories through the long lens of time gave them clarity. Valor could not recall Germayne encountering a mate, a lover, or life partner of any sort. If he had done so, he'd kept it private. Had seeing his brother-in-arms find his true love and his true calling made Germayne bitter? Jealous?

It seemed too simple. GerMayne au Coyne, the great Warlock, pushed to darkness and vengeance out of jealousy? The coincidence of their parting and the simultaneous rise of the Némesati began to toll like a bell in Valor's mind, and possibly, put a sword in his hand.

*

Darcy leaned against the wall of the enclosure, her face in her hands. The last several hours blurred together in a mind-numbing mishmash of real versus unreal, sane versus insane. Aware of time moving forward, yet standing still. Interminable hours of isolation and darkness had turned their prison into a tomb of sensory deprivation for both women, and its only release the touch and taste and scent of each other. Whether she enjoyed it or not, Darcy would never be able to forget the taste of another woman.

She could no longer tell whether it might be day or night, whether she was hungry or thirsty. All that mattered was to escape before total dementia set in. Shania's withdrawal symptoms had worsened, turning the blond nymph into a squalling, helpless, sweating ball of flesh whose caterwauling refused to cease. She'd all but given up trying to communicate with her, listening instead to the monotonous beat of Shania's head striking the wall.

Darcy wanted her mother. She wanted out of this place, out of her head, and safely back in her happy life before all of this pain began. If only she could talk to her now, like they used to, without words. Perhaps her mom would come find her, take her home and make everything all right again the way only mothers know to do.

Shania began to utter truncated shrieks each time her skull made contact. Clinging to the last vestiges of control, Darcy made one last attempt to get through to her, make her stop her senseless self-mutilation.

"Shania. Let's play a game."

Bang. Shriek. Bang. Shriek. Bang. No shriek.

"Let's play a game," Darcy repeated, into the brief interval of silence.

"A game," Shania said, testing the word in her mouth like a new food.

"Yes, a game. It's called, uh, 'because.' I ask a question, and you answer with the word 'because' in front of it. Then you ask a question, and I answer with 'because.' Do you understand?"

Shania didn't respond, but Darcy took that to at least mean she was listening. "I'll start. Why did you end up at Dr.McCaine's? Remember, start with because."

The head-pounding stopped. "Because I was sick."

"Good. Now it's your turn to ask."

"Why did you have sex with Dr. McCaine?"

"Because I'm in love with him. Why were you sick?"

"Because he gave me injections."

Good, Darcy thought. This was getting somewhere. "Your turn again."

"Why do you have a cat?"

"Because my mother gave her to me. She can't look after her any more. Why do you call him 'he' and not his name?"

"Because I hate his name."

"Why not call him Bill, or Frank?"

"That's two questions. You stole my turn."

"Ah-ah, you forgot to start with because."

Shania huffed. "Because his name isn't Bill or Frank. It's Germayne. Why are we playing this game?"

Darcy froze. Germayne. Not a common name. In fact she'd never heard that name until her mother said it, and this…this…beast that held them captive is called Germayne? She willed what remained of her mind not to make the next leap, but it jumped there nevertheless. A powerful warlock named Germayne was her father. "Because I want you to stop hurting yourself and help me find a way out of here."

*

"Let's fly, cousin. Get this done."

Germayne set down his fifth glass of Scotch and licked his lips. "Anxious, are we?" He slapped his knees and stood up. "You're right…it's time. The reinforcements have arrived and the force field is down."

"Reinforcements?" Lucie asked, anger rising in her voice. "You never mentioned this before. Germayne, you continually refuse to divulge the entire plan to me! Do you not trust me? Why does anyone else need to be involved?"

From the very fiber of the walls came Germayne's loyals, witches and warlocks of every stripe, every country. Many of them Lucie knew, and others she did not. They materialized

from the windows, wallpaper, furniture and fireplaces.
She counted at least twenty souls, among then FarRell, a
particularly narcissistic warlock with whom she'd had a brief
flirtation. All talk, no substance, with his long, cinnamon-
colored hair and angelic facial features. He moved forward
to speak a few private words with Germayne. She also
spotted AraLyn, a brunette giantess with an Amazon-like
physique and ego to match. These were the legionnaires in
his little game of conquest.

"Every battle must have a strategy, cousin. If the front
lines, that would be you, fail or lose heart during the
campaign, we should have regiments at our flanks, yes?
Come. We must go."

Like a flock of ravens, they swirled in formation and took
to the sky in bird fashion, Germayne in the lead. It had been
a long time since Lucie herself had flown. Hadn't been much
call for it when one could apparate anywhere they wished.

Even though flying in a large group made it more difficult
to hit a target destination in such close proximity to each
other, she admired the drama of it. The harsh night wind
rushed through her hair that had turned to glossy gray and
black feathers for the duration of the flight. Her sequined
black cloak formed her wingspan, and her fingernails became
talons of destruction as she soared with purpose alongside
the others.

The lights of Boston glittered below them, and the
starless, indigo sky arced down to skim the waters of the
harbour and touch the horizon beyond. Lucie felt exhilarated
in a way she did not expect. Her desire for blood, revenge,
and victory filled her veins and radiated out through her
bird's eyes and ears.

Like a black rain, they descended upon the street where
McCaine's Pharmacy stood, their feet touching down light

as angels onto the cobbled pavement. Their feathery features
resumed human form as they circled the building.

"Lucie and I will go inside. The rest of you wait out here,
cover the entrances and exits. I don't anticipate we'll be
long," Germayne said, his saw-toothed grin flashing white
even in the umbra of night. He seemed over-confident,
more so than usual, and this worried Lucie. Valor knew
they were coming, and he'd had time to plan a defense.
But there remained one element of surprise. Valor wouldn't
be expecting her at Germayne's side. She raised the hem
of her cape, and with the swooping gesture of a matador,
disappeared from the street.

Chapter Eighteen

Darcy's fingers inched along the dirt wall, feeling for any kind of fissure, frame or latch that might yield a clue to the structure and mechanics of the time-out room. Shania did the same, starting in the opposite direction so that they would meet when they completed the perimeter of the room.

"We'll never get out of here," Shania whined. "I told you. Not until he lets us out."

"Just keep going," Darcy said. "Doing anything is better than crying about it. What's the longest you've ever been in here?"

Shania snorted, trying to keep her runny nose in check. Darcy thought she almost preferred the sound of her head-banging to the soggy, congested whiffs she now uttered. Their groping hands found each other's in the dark, bringing their search path to an end.

"I don't know. Hours. Days. After awhile, it didn't matter. I would just go to sleep." She sank to the floor with a whumping sound. "This is useless."

Darcy began to agree. However, they had air to breathe;

there must be an inlet somewhere. "What would happen when you went to sleep?"

After a moment, Shania answered. "I would wake up in my room."

Darcy rubbed her eyes with both hands. She could use some sleep herself. She had no idea how long she'd been awake. Somehow, sleep seemed akin to giving up and surrendering to their captor. But she didn't know how much longer she could cling to sanity, much less consciousness, in this place. Dammit. Shania's 'craft had to be of some use. *Think.*

"What did you think about when you went to sleep? Did you have dreams?"

More silence. Darcy gave her a shake. "What did you think about?"

"I cried myself to sleep. Wishing it would all be a dream."

An abstract, absurd thought came to Darcy. "What if is a dream?" she wondered aloud. "What if all this is like…a hologram? You watch Star Trek?"

"Star what?"

"A hologram, a digitized, three-dimensional projection built with laser optics. Looks real, feels real, as long as you believe it's real. But when you know it's not real…" Darcy scrambled to her feet, grabbing Shania by the arm and forcing her up.

"What now? Leave me alone, I'm tired."

"Yeah, me too. Close your eyes. Think about your room. Think about waking up from a dream, nothing else. Just that, and walk with me."

Darcy moved them forward in slow steps. She concentrated on her mom's house in sunny Phoenix, where she would be at semester break, surrounded by the smells of roast turkey and gravy. She imagined her grandma at the piano, the keys moving though her fingers never touched them. Another step. Candles lit at the dinner table, red and tartan linens, crisp white wine being poured. Another step, and another, the ground softening beneath her feet. Fresh air caressed her damp face, and sunlight warmed her eyelids.

"Oh," Shania gasped, and stumbled from Darcy's grasp. Darcy opened her eyes, and blinked painfully in the sudden bright light streaming in through a window. Shania lay crying on the carpeted floor of a pink and white room, running her fingers across the nubbled fibers of the rug. "I'm home, I'm home," she blubbered between sobs.

Darcy exhaled in relief. Her crazy hunch had worked. Despite having the appearance of a life-sized Barbie playhouse, this must be Shania's room, and within it the portal to the "time-out" room, in reality a hologram projection studio. She flopped on the ruffled pink bedspread and lapsed into slumber.

*

Altan Sibelius awoke with a jerking motion of his head, the same as when he would nod off in his favorite armchair at home. But the monotonous hiss of a respirator and the bleach-boiled smell of hospital sheets told him he lay in a different place altogether. The room sat in semi-darkness and the door to the hall partially closed. Occasional footsteps passed by.

In his heart, he knew the professionals here would be unable to help him. His diseases layered upon one another, brought to full blown status with the insidious progress of the unnamed virus. He hoped that McCaine had found and understood his documentation and took the necessary items from his office to prepare the *Sanguis Prima*. He also hoped he would not be too far gone before McCaine could return and administer the serum.

He couldn't shake the terror he'd felt when the 'visitor,'

as he'd taken to calling him, had invaded his mind and body. It was unlike anything he'd ever experienced, and he'd experienced a lot in his seventy years. This one he wouldn't care to repeat. He inhaled a ragged breath through his congested airways, triggering another severe bout of coughing. Among other afflictions, his emphysema had grown the most acute. He groped for the call button hidden beneath the rumpled bedding.

He lay back and closed his eyes, the spasms subsiding somewhat as he listened for the approach of an attendant. He waited a minute or two, but heard no sound other than the machinery around him. A sudden tingling of his flesh snapped his eyes open again, and he shouted in fright just as a cool, firm hand closed over his lips.

The man's face was unfamiliar to him, but seemed young enough to be one of his students. Parted in the middle, his shoulder-length hair was the color of cinnamon, and his handsome face dimpled into a curious smile as he pressed it close to Altan's.

"Having trouble breathing, Professor?" His grin stretched wider. "Must be all this nasty technology." He reached out his other hand, and with a snapping motion silenced all the electronic equipment at his bedside. "There. That's better."

Altan struggled to free himself, grasping at the hand that clamped his mouth and nose shut, blocking off his last channels of air. The man's grip felt unnaturally strong, and the terror building in the pit of Altan's stomach spread upward to his brain. As consciousness left him, he heard two words.

"Goodnight, Professor."

*

Valor sat in his armchair, waiting. He felt the witches' presence outside, their web of hatred tightening around his world. He didn't expect so many of them. Trust Germayne to not fight fair, the coward. A private army of sorcerers against one defenseless warlock. How would that look in the 'craft industry papers tomorrow? A bitter laugh escaped his lips. Defenseless, he may be. But not unprepared.

A gust of wind rattled the windowpanes, and he rose from his chair to stand in the center of the room near his examining couch. In the next second, two figures apparated near him, one in front and one behind. The one that faced him caught him by surprise.

Lucie.

She lunged at him, her raven's talons cocked and ready to cut him to bloody shreds. Valor stood his ground, bracing for her attack. With a steady glare, he cast a suspension charm around her, slowing her momentum as she struck, enabling him to grab her wrists and throw her to the floor. She gnashed her teeth at him, kicked her feet and bucked her hips, but he held her down like a wrestling opponent.

He sensed Germayne lurking at his back. He clamped both of Lucie's wrists with one hand while reaching into his pocket with the other. He pulled out the syringe and plunged it into her neck, emptying the chamber with a quick stroke of his thumb.

Her screams of rage shattered every beaker and flask in his laboratory. He rolled off her and got to his feet. Germayne stared at him from about two meters away, his arms folded and leaning in a casual stance as though bothered with neither Lucie's predicament nor Valor's offensive maneuver.

"Where are Darcy and Shania?" Valor demanded.

"They are no longer a concern of yours," Germayne said. "Is that the best you could come up with? A needle?" He gestured with an open palm to the syringe in Valor's hand.

"Show me they are all right and I won't need to fight you."

"Who said anything about fighting? The message was quite clear, I thought. Give yourself up, or they will both die."

Valor stepped back, spreading his arms wide and tossing the hypo away. It landed in the corner with a faint tinkle. "Well, here I am. I surrender. Come and get me." A corner of his mouth curled up in a malevolent grin.

Germayne began to stalk him in a wide circle. Lucie squirmed on the floor, holding her hands to her neck. "What did you just shoot into me," she growled.

"You'll find out," Valor said, keeping his eyes on Germayne. "Show me that Darcy and Shania are safe, and then you're free to kill me. Stab me, curse me, I don't much care how you do it. Just let the girls go."

Germayne's expression turned amused. "You don't read between the lines very well, do you? I never said they would be let go. I only said they would both die if you didn't give yourself up."

Valor saw Lucie scramble up, bracing herself against the divan where the two of them had fucked each other barely a week before. What a difference a week could make.

"Hurry up and do it, cousin. I can't stand to look at him another minute," Lucie said, with gravel in her voice.

"Your plan is to kill them whether I surrender or not, is it? Well, then. Not much motivation for me to come quietly is there?" Valor raised his palms to the air, and mirrored Germayne's circling movements. So, before you do away with me old man, I have a few questions."

"Really," Germayne said, squinting his eyes. "Last requests for the condemned man, eh? Sorry, the kitchen is closed for the evening. I'm afraid your last meal won't be forthcoming."

"I'm not the one who's hungry," Valor retorted. "But you are. Hungry for what? Power? Domination? Self-aggrandizement? What do those bring you? Once you have them, what will you feel? Happiness? Satisfaction? Somehow I doubt it."

"Shut up, little brother. You have no concept of what I want, what I plan to do. You have always thought so small… it has been your undoing. Always thinking of others and casting away your power and your knowledge upon the great unwashed. Sickening! You had everything going for you, yet you wasted it all on philanthropic nonsense."

"Germayne!" Lucie shouted. "You're wasting time. Don't listen to all his analytic bullshit. Kill the fucker."

Germayne rounded on her. "When I want your mouth open, I will unzip my pants, is that clear, you cock-addled little tramp?" He crooked his elbow, showing the back of his hand to her. Lucie fell back, choking.

Valor glanced back and forth between them. "That's no way to treat a lady, Germayne. Much less your own cousin. I'll bet that's it, isn't it? You've never known a woman in the true sense have you, you hollow bastard. You're a sorry excuse even for a man. And you call yourself a Warlock." Valor snorted in disdain. "I know what you plan to do, and why. You couldn't stand to see me prosper, go beyond your aspirations. Knowing you could never go there yourself."

Germayne whirled to face him. "You talk too much, boy. I'd like to hear how you would sound without your tongue!" He made a scissor symbol with his fingers.

Anticipating his move, Valor cast a shielding charm to deflect Germayne's spell. "You telegraph your intentions, old man. Losing your edge? You'd never make it in a boxing ring!"

"Enough. Say goodbye to all you know, mac Haine."

Valor watched as through the walls and windows came

Germayne's minions, impatient with keeping sentry outside. Witches and warlocks, young and old. He could feel them in varying stages of sickness. No wonder they followed Germayne — clinging to the promise of salvation.

"Fine," Valor shouted. "Deny it. See where it gets you. All your power, all that you hope to control, will mean nothing in the face of your loneliness." He panned the faces of his attackers as they closed in on him. "Is this whom you choose to follow? A lonely, embittered old soul who commands your loyalty only out of fear? He lies to you. He is not the only one who can save you. Kill me, and you kill your chance at freedom."

Chapter Nineteen

Darcy squeezed the plunger, transporting the needed drug into Shania's arm. The girl shuddered and hung her head as the chemicals raced into her starving system. High or not, she needed Shania's skills in 'craft to accomplish their next steps. "There now. Feel better?"

Shania looked up, rapturous. "You're beautiful," she whispered.

Darcy's insides gave a sharp twist. The intimate moments she'd shared with Shania would be indelibly etched in her consciousness. She hadn't expected to feel this way about another woman. But she could bury her feelings very deep. "Don't get carried away. We were just helping each other through a rough patch, okay?" She withdrew the syringe and tossed it into a wastebasket.

Shania looked at her with a blank, surreal expression on her face. It would do as a yes. They'd rested and changed into some of Shania's clothes. Darcy wore a tee shirt and jeans while Shania insisted on a dress. "Because it's pretty," she'd explained.

"Can you take us to Valor's pharmacy?" Darcy coaxed.

A smile and a nod came from the girl. "Okay. Tell me what I need to do."

Shania embraced Darcy in a flower-child hug. "Hold on to me," she whispered. In a few heartbeats they stood inside the back entrance of McCaine's Pharmacy. The sensation of teleportation exhilarated Darcy. She wished she'd inherited this skill. The reassembling of her molecules in a trans-dimensional state left her with renewed strength rather than fatigue.

The two women skipped up the staircase to Valor's office. When they reached the entrance door, Shania balked. "What's the problem?" Darcy asked. "C'mon, now's not the time to turn chickenshit."

"There's too many of them," Shania breathed in a wispy, dreamlike tone. "They will sense us…better turn back."

"What do you mean? Who's in there?"

"Witches and Warlocks. From many places. They're surrounding Valor…"

Darcy's main thought had been to return to Oliviah, but now she grew fearful at Shania's words. The situation had changed. "We've got to help him, then. Open the door," Darcy urged.

"He's there, too. Germayne." Shania's nerves got the best of her, and she began to hyperventilate. "He'll kill me for sure when he sees I've escaped." She crouched with her back to the wall, unwilling to go further.

"All right, stay here. I'm going in." Darcy twisted the knob without making a sound and slid inside the room. The evil *kathra* filled her nostrils instantly, almost knocking her down in its intensity — the same one she'd sensed from the Horse Head game piece, and again at the conference. She crept against the wall of Valor's office and ducked behind his desk. She heard voices in the outer room, all garbled together as if communing in an ancient chant.

One voice rang out above the others. "Don't you see? My death will not solve anything. The healing has already begun. Look at her." Darcy recognized Valor's commanding tones among the cacophony. His death? Panic rose in her chest.

"He lies. It's a placebo, nothing more. Will you all wager your lives on the word of a liar, trying to save his own skin?"

This new voice struck Darcy's heart like a bass chord. She pressed a fist to her chest, calming its thudding. The time had come to reach out, gamble on her instincts. Summoning her psychic lines of communication she'd so cherished between herself and her family, she called out. "*Father.*"

A ripple of silence cut through the angry hubbub.

"*Who is this?*" came the response.

"*Father,*" she repeated. The *kathra* moved toward her inside her mind, and along with it the truth of his identity. She could hide from him no longer. She rose from behind Valor's desk and ventured a few steps forward, enough to see into the next room. The scene she beheld seemed out of a horror movie. At least twenty individuals stood, paced, or levitated in a menacing circle around Valor. He held his ground, his piercing violet eyes settling on her as she came into view. She felt small and insignificant in the face of all the witchly firepower before her. The very air crackled with supernatural force.

One tall figure stood out from the crowd, seeming to expand in all dimensions as he floated in midair and turned to face her, the effect both terrifying and mesmerizing. "*You,*" he said, the single word reverberating in her brain until her temples throbbed in pain. "*How is it you speak to me, mortal?*"

The waves of wordless telepathy drilled her to her knees in his presence. "*I am not quite mortal. And not quite witch. My mother is Audra deHavalend.*"

The group of onlookers appeared listless and confused

as their leader turned away from them to focus his attention elsewhere. Valor stood wary in their midst. The Warlock who was her father looked down upon her with something wavering between hatred and disbelief. She could vaguely recognize the strong line of his chin that reflected in her own face every time she looked in a mirror. Though hardened with age, Darcy acknowledged the striking good looks that would have turned a woman's head in days gone by.

"AuDra du Avalon is dead. How dare you evoke her name."

She'd hit a soft spot, and noted Germayne's altered pronunciation of Audra's name. As much as she could not imagine this frightening, saturnine monster together with her mother, it became plain he had feelings for her. *"She lives still. She kept me a secret from you, to protect me."*

"You lie. You will be dead soon enough and your lies dead with you."

"Are you not curious how I escaped your trap, Germayne?"

His expression clouded, but his eyes burned with a green fire that she'd never seen the likes of. *"You know my name."*

"Of course. Mother told me. Well? About your trap. Not so spiffy. I figured it out. Why are you here? Why are you threatening Doctor McCaine?"

"It does not concern you, but perhaps you'd like to share in his fate? Yes, I can feel your attraction to him. Fine. Even better if he sees you die before his eyes." Aloud he said, "Come out. Stand beside him." Germayne gestured to the group that hovered, stalked, perched in a circle all around Valor.

"No!" Valor shouted. "Leave her out of this."

Germayne rotated in his floating position to face him. "Why not bring her to your side? A moment ago you said you wanted to see her safe. Now you will. *Come, child.*"

Darcy's limbs began to move, free of her own volition. She entered the main room, aware of all the witches' eyes upon her. Among them were the red lasers of the sorceress who'd kidnapped her. Darcy held her gaze, sending a message of recognition and of hatred. The sorceress' black hair with gray streaks seemed to move and undulate, as alive as the rest of her body. Something seemed different though. The sorceress' skin had lost its pallor from their previous encounter. Her ruby lips seemed not so red, and plumped with dewy moisture. Almost soft and caring. Darcy admired the black cloak draped around her. The exotic fabric sparkled in a random pattern like stars glinting against the night sky.

Into the circle of witches and warlocks she passed until her body came to a stop next to Valor. The tractor spell released, and Valor caught her as she slumped to the floor.

"Darcy," he whispered. "Are you all right? I'm sorry I wasn't here, so sorry you had to become involved." His voice stretched tight with despair and regret.

Being in his arms again seemed worth every minute of torture she'd experienced. If she was truly to die she wanted it to be here, with him, in his embrace. "Yes I'm all right. So is Shania," she said, in the quietest voice possible. If she kept Shania's presence unknown, she might be able to help them. That is, if she could stop cowering in the hallway. "What is going on…I don't understand this. My father wants to kill you. Why?"

"Father?" Valor questioned, his face registering shock.

Darcy nodded with an almost imperceptible tilt of her chin. "I told you I would ask. It's a long story. He doesn't seem to care. He doesn't believe me anyway."

Germayne floated high above the group, watching over them.

"What do we do now?" asked one of the warlocks. "This is a change of plans."

AraLyn spoke up, addressing Germayne. "How do you respond to VaLor's statements? He says you are not the only source of the cure. Have you lied to us, as he's conjectured?"

Tittering waves of dissent passed over the entourage. Germayne's countenance turned fierce, his bodily manifestation growing larger as his rage mounted. He raised both arms, then brought them down in a silencing gesture. All of them, with the exception of the sorceress, fell back. Some of the witches screamed and clutched at their bodies as they writhed in agony.

Darcy watched as the horrific affectations took place around the room. Skins turned black, open sores oozed blood and mucous; eyeballs rolled up to show hideous whites. They all had the virus, she realized, their individual genetic weaknesses stimulated by the infection and accelerated by Germayne's spell. He held them helpless in his power. She felt sickened at the thought of his blood running through her veins.

Mother was right to have spurned him and cut him out of their lives. Her last desperate thoughts focused into a tight beam directed at Audra.

"Mother, help us."

*

Lucie watched as the others collapsed in pain and suffering. She was no stranger to Germayne's cruelty, but seeing this misery inflicted on so many others made her heart grow cold. A quick inventory showed FarRell was not among them. It struck her also, that she herself stood aside, unharmed. This raised her consciousness to a new level. Did Germayne trust her enough to leave her out of this attack on the group, or had something else transpired? Some other reason she'd been excused?

She touched her neck, where Valor's hypodermic had

entered her. "You'll find out," he'd said. She crouched down, not wanting to call attention to herself. She not only felt untouched by Germayne's spell, but her strength and vitality returning even more than it had since her sexual epiphany in her bathtub.

He'd done it, she said to herself. Valor found the cure, and chose to give it to her even as she tried to murder him where he stood. Valor did care. She glanced over at him, holding the girl protectively in his arms. Perhaps he did not love Lucie in the way she wanted; but he loved her enough to save her, and sacrifice himself.

A single, undisputed thought swelled in her mind. *Germayne must die.*

Lucie tried to catch Valor's attention when he looked her way. She touched the spot on her neck and sent him a questioning look. His eyes softened, and gave a single, deliberate nod. The knowledge gave her satisfaction, but did not present a way to get to Germayne. He held each of them captive in their personal torment of disease.

Surely all of them together could defeat Germayne, if she could communicate what Valor told them as truth. Then as suddenly as he'd gripped them, Germayne released the others from his stranglehold of torture. He'd apparently made his point.

"Now. Any other questions? Or are you all quite through?" Germayne looked around at the circle of faces, some glowering, some fearful, some expressionless.

"We didn't agree to kill a young girl," said a voice. "Or a helpless old man."

Lucie twisted around to determine who spoke. FarRell had just joined them, standing outside the ring of bodies. Where had he been?

"Who is she?" FarRell pointed to Darcy. "Is she mortal? Let her go," he said.

"No. She knows too much," Lucie piped up. She wasn't sure what made her say it, but the fringes of a plan formed in her mind. "And besides, she's mine to kill. I captured her. She's been a thorn in my side too long already." Lucie flashed Valor a warning look.

He returned her stare, and surreptitiously touched his back pocket. Suddenly she understood. He'd had two syringes prepared. One to cure. And one to kill.

"How about it, Germayne? Give her to me, I'll save you the trouble. The others need not have her death on their conscience," Lucie continued.

Grumbling agreement sounded from the group. Germayne relaxed his position and floated down to floor level. "Very well. Dispose of her, Lu. Take her away."

Lucie stood and approached the two figures in the centre of the room. Darcy looked fearful, her eyes darting from Lucie, to Germayne, to Valor and back again. She clung tighter to Valor, refusing to move. "Get away from me, bitch!"

"Oh save it. Time's up, Goldilocks," Lucie said, holding her hand out.

Valor kept his grip on Darcy. "Germayne. Would you have your own daughter murdered? Do your followers know that you have no morals, no compunctions, no integrity whatsoever? That you will turn on them the minute they've done your bidding?"

Murmurs of surprise echoed from the collective group. Lucie stopped dead in her tracks. *Daughter?* He never said anything about a daughter. As her elder cousin, she'd known Germayne all of her long, long lifetime and never once had he presented a consort or partner of any kind. She hadn't thought it strange until now. How could he have fathered this curly-headed mortal? This was too much. Then the most crushing thought of all came to Lucie.

If it were true, this immature, red-haired pain in the ass that she'd been jealous of, forced to kidnap and nearly kill, was her own flesh and blood, too. Her second cousin.

Chapter Twenty

Shania huddled on the landing outside Valor's office. The entranceway had grown cold. She sat rubbing her arms and legs for warmth, taking care to avoid the painful red lesions that had multiplied since her arrival. Her breath came short, and she rocked her head side to side. Suddenly, a figure apparated below her, at ground level. The woman looked around as if unfamiliar with the place. She appeared to be about seventy, yet stood tall and walked without difficulty. She began to climb the stairs when she spotted Shania.

"What are you doing up there?" the woman asked. "Are you lost?" She advanced another step or two.

"No," Shania answered, shivering. "Are you?"

"I don't think so. I'm looking for Darcy deHavalend. Do you know her? She is supposed to be here."

"She's inside. I don't think you want to go in there."

The woman smiled a grim smile. "Yes. I think I do. Excuse me." She moved up the stairs past Shania, then hesitated with her hand on the door latch. "Are you sick?" she asked. "You don't look well. Perhaps you'd better come in with me."

"I...I...I'm not sure I can," Shania whimpered.

"Looks like you've been out here for some time. It can't be healthy, so come."

The woman reached down and grasped Shania beneath her elbow. Shania stood up, her legs shaky from crouching for so long. Before she could twist the latch, Shania gestured with one finger upright against her lips.

The woman nodded, and pushed the door open.

Voices, in varying levels of volume, emanated from inside. The two women passed through the office area until they could get a clear view of the area beyond. As they edged closer, Shania stopped to lean on Valor's desk. The woman turned to look at her, and Shania shook her head, unable to go on. She pulled away from her grasp and hid under the desk.

The woman didn't argue this time. She moved without sound toward the commotion in the other room.

"Is this true?" Lucie demanded.

"She lies. She claims her mother to be someone long dead." Germayne roared.

"Not so dead, Germayne."

All eyes turned to this new voice, and the accompanying figure that had slipped in unnoticed and stood at the edge of the room. Her graying hair still showed traces of red-blond; her face tracked with wrinkles that bespoke of someone much older than her stature suggested. The only one not looking at her was Germayne, who stood unmoving, with his back to her.

"Mom!" Darcy yelled, and broke free of Valor's hold, dashing past Lucie to reach her mother's side. Tears streamed down her face as she hugged the woman's tall, thin frame. "I wasn't sure you would hear me."

Germayne at last turned around to face them. "AuDra,"

he said, his commanding voice pared down to a whisper. He seemed to have no other words.

"Yes, it's me. Yes, she's your daughter. I never wanted you to know about her. What is going on here?" she asked in disdain, taking in the gathering of her long-forgotten kinsmen.

"AuDra," murmured several witches.

Germayne stood agape, his intent seemingly forgotten in the face of this unexpected bombshell. Those seconds were all Valor needed. With everyone distracted, he lunged at Germayne, drawing the second hypo from his pocket and jamming it into his neck.

The room erupted in a frenzy of witches and warlocks surging forward and knocking Valor off his feet. His head hit the floor, and he felt his limbs seized and the weight of several bodies holding him down.

"What did you do?" one of them screamed.

"Should have killed him while we had the chance," growled another. "We're all going to die now, thanks to him."

Germayne fell to his knees, pawing at the injection site where the syringe still protruded from his flesh. He ripped it out and tossed it aside.

"Stop!" Lucie screeched, above the din of voices and scrambling bodies. "Let Valor up…none of you will have to die! He told you the truth! He has the serum to cure us. We don't need Germayne. Let him go."

"You stupid cow! You're so in love with McCaine you'd say anything to save him," AraLyn said. "We've got no proof he has the cure, either. What's happening to Germayne? What if he's our only chance?"

Germayne fell forward from his kneeling stance, landing on his face right in front of Darcy and Audra. His body jerked in a few involuntary spasms, then lay still. Audra

looked away, while Darcy crouched down and reached out
a tentative hand to touch his head. "What did you give him,
Val?" Her voice lacked any emotion.

The group forced Valor to his feet, still holding him
in a full nelson. "Some of his own medicine. Literally.
That hypo had a super-concentrated form of the Némesati,
combined with nightshade and enough Thiopental to take
out half the prisoners on death row." He struggled to free
his arms. "Don't you all understand?" he said to the crowd.
"Germayne created the virus, from his own blood. That's
why he was immune, and that's why he also had the cure.
He's played you all for fools, and nearly killed you all in the
process." He turned to Darcy, his voice softening. "I'm sorry,
Darcy. I didn't know he was your father until you told me
just now. I'd planned to kill him all along."

She sat in silence, stroking the ridges of Germayne's
forehead in what seemed like absent fascination. Audra knelt
beside her. "It's all right," Darcy said. "You've slain the
monster and freed the people."

Lucie spoke up. "She's right! It doesn't matter about
Germayne. Valor found the cure, he shot me with it before all
of you arrived. Look at me!" She flung her arm in a circular
motion, and the very foundations of the building shook and
shuddered until she dropped her arm to make it stop.

"We can test LuSie's blood," Valor said. "In my lab here.
You'll see the virus has been eradicated. I've made enough
serum for most of you, but I'll need help in preparing
more." They released him, and he rushed to Darcy. He
knelt down beside her and Audra, Germayne's lifeless form
already beginning to decompose from the effects of the drug
concoction. "Forgive me," he said, to both Darcy and her
mother.

A pitiful wail echoed from the direction of Valor's office.
Objects fell to the ground as a figure stumbled forward,

her eyes wild, hair in tangles and blood dripping from the multitude of sores covering the exposed parts of her body.

"Shania," Darcy said, tears filling her eyes. Valor got to his feet and hurried to grab hold of the tortured girl. Her eyes rolled up into her eyelids as she passed out in his arms.

*

Valor carried Shania her to the bathroom and laid her in the tub, stripped off her clothing summoned the flow of water from the tap with a wave of his finger.

Darcy and Audra hovered at the door to the bathroom. "Is she going to die?" Audra asked. "Can you save her?"

Valor didn't answer right away. "Darcy," he said, with his back turned to them. "Can you wash her while I get the serum ready?"

"Yes, of course," Darcy said, and stepped forward to grab a washcloth from the stack of clean linens on the shelf. She knelt beside Valor at the edge of the tub, expecting him to move aside while she worked. He seemed frozen there, clutching Shania's wet dress in his hands. Darcy looked at him in concern. His handsome features contorted with pain and emotion.

"I didn't protect her. I should have watched her more carefully. I've failed her."

"Not yet. Go, get the serum, now! It's not too late," Darcy urged. "She's tougher than you think." She remembered one of their earlier arguments. "Be a scientist, now."

He looked at her with hollowed, broken eyes, their amethyst glow almost extinguished. Then he left the room.

*

Hours passed after Valor gave Shania her injection. She lay unconscious, her vitals low. Darcy sat at her bedside, watching the monitors, dabbing the sores as they healed. She heard a noise at the door.

A young warlock stood there, the one that had argued for her life. "Need a break?" he asked.

Darcy put down the cloth she'd been using, and exhaled. "Yeah." She stood and stretched, as he walked over to the bed. She rubbed her eyes, and truly saw him for the first time. Quite handsome, she thought, with his cinnamon-colored hair and curvy lips that begged to be kissed.

"Name's FarRell," he said.

She nodded. "Darcy."

"Yeah, I know. What's your connection to her," he asked, pointing to Shania.

Darcy smirked, unsure how to answer. She really didn't know how to describe it herself. "We have the same doctor," she finally said, then chuckled and left the room.

She found Valor in his lab, working alongside Lucie and several other volunteers to produce more serum. He looked up when she came near. "Looks like your blood is fine. Both our cultures showed zero growth." He wore a weary smile. "Well done, Dr. Johnson."

"Glad to be of service, Dr. Masters. You look exhausted, why don't you get some rest? I think we've got the routine down now," she said, gesturing to the crew of pinch-hit first aiders surrounding him.

"I should go and see Altan," he said. "He's probably more susceptible than anybody, given his age. I'm not sure how the mortal metabolism will fight the virus. I have no data on that."

Darcy pursed her lips in acknowledgment. "True. How about I go instead?"

Valor smiled. "See. I told you you'd be a good nurse." He handed her a plastic medikit.

She shook her head. "I think I'd be a good doctor," she

replied, taking the kit in one hand, and reaching out for his with the other. "C'mon, bed now."

He clasped her hand and walked out from behind the lab counter. "Whatever you say, Dr. Masters."

She led him to his bedroom and closed the door. He took off his shirt, and prepared to undo his belt when he realized she hadn't left the room. "I thought you prescribed rest," he said.

"I said bed," she corrected, and moved to stand in front of him. She took hold of his belt buckle in her own hands and continued undressing him. He seemed too tired to resist. When she'd gotten his pants off, she gave him a gentle push that sent him flopping onto the bed.

"Darcy. I'm not sure we have time."

"Depends," she purred, leaning over him and gliding her hands up his naked thighs. "On what service you choose. I do offer an express version…" her voice trailed off as her lips hovered near his exposed cock. She gave it a lick. He laid his head back and groaned.

She'd never given a blow job before. Somehow it seemed right, under the circumstances. She'd read enough pulp novels to understand the basics plus a few variations. She held the base of his upright shaft in one hand, and licked the sides of it like a soft-serve cone. Her tongue glided over his warm skin, lingering over every bump and ridge of veins, exploring them like a road map.

He groaned again. "That is sweet torture," he said.

"Take it like a doctor," she murmured, and continued her way up to the reddened plum of the head, the soft skin stretched tight over its curves. Her tongue circled under its ridge, then overtop, licking up the glistening drop of pre-cum that had appeared. Sticky and salty, Darcy lifted it on the tip of her tongue, tiny crystal strings clinging between. She took the whole head in her mouth, her lips raking its domelike surface up and down, in and out. Then she sucked, harder than she'd ever sucked anything in her life. His cock filled the roof of her mouth, her tongue pressing it hard against her palate, taking steady, strong pulses.

"Holy fuck," she heard him say, felt his hands touch either side of her head, grasping handfuls of her strawberry locks between his fingers and pulling her down on him. She kept up the sucking rhythm for a few more pulses, then slackened her jaw to take all of him in.

She let his hands guide her head up and down, forward and back, allowing his thick shaft to slide in and out with ease. Each stroke forward she tried to push a little more, allowing the tip of his penis to venture further down her throat.

"Ohh, that's it, baby," he murmured, "that's so good, that's so fucking good…"

She picked up the pace, feeling his pelvis start to drive forward with each of her strokes, his hands pulling on her hair enough that it hurt. His cock felt rock hard against the soft tissues of her mouth, growing larger, rougher. She backed off, positioning him so that she could repeat the sucking motion, pulling hard.

"Fuck!" he said aloud, and filled her mouth with cum, its bitter tang flooding her taste buds. She knew to swallow, so relaxed her throat and drank him in. She felt the waves of precious liquid cascade past her tongue and flow warmly down her insides. The sensation was new, but the idea of consuming this man gave her a satisfaction beyond measure. The muscles of his cock twitched and pulsed as his seed spilled into her, gradually subsiding as he recovered.

Darcy swallowed the last drops of him, then withdrew him from her mouth in a slow pass. His breathing decelerated, and he released his hold on her hair, stroking the top of her head gently.

"Just what the doctor ordered," he said, a satisfied smile on his face. "I think you've perfected that procedure."

She kissed the top of his cock, and wriggled off the bed. "Sleep now, that's an order."

Chapter Twenty One

Visiting hours at the hospital were almost over. Darcy forced herself to hurry to Professor Sibelius' ward. She'd been awake for nearly two days, but pasted a big smile on her face in hopes of cheering the old man up if he wasn't doing so well. She found the room, and stepped in. The privacy curtain hung drawn around his bed. She realized he might be sleeping, and approached on tiptoe, taking a tentative peek around the edge of the light blue drape.

An empty bed greeted her. An almost physical stab of pain ripped through her gut, her mind not wanting to accept what her eyes were telling her. No! They were too late! An anguished moan rose from her lungs and she took a step backward, almost tripping over a guest chair, then sinking into it in despair and defeat.

"Ma'am?" A nurse appeared at the door. "Are you all right?"

Darcy looked up, still in shock. "The professor?" she asked weakly.

An expression of recognition formed in the nurse's dark

features. "Ah, Mr. Sibelius….he's now in room 520, two doors down."

Darcy collapsed in relief. "Thank you," she said, hoisting herself from the chair. The medikit jostled in her pocket, but the nurse had already moved on down the hall. She walked quietly into 520. The professor was indeed sleeping, his hands folded atop a men's magazine on his lap and his head resting to one side. Snoring.

She stood there just watching him, glad he was alive, when he awoke in mid-snore. His head snapped up, and immediately began coughing. Darcy went to his bedside and offered him his water cup with the bendie straw. When he'd calmed down, he took one look at her and said, "You've come back to flirt with me some more, eh? Well, what McCaine doesn't know won't hurt him."

Darcy laughed, and held the water cup for him to take a few sips. "Well, he does know, actually. He wanted to come himself but I offered instead." She noted the absence of a respirator. Apparently he'd improved enough to do away with it.

"Even better. Is he planning to stop by later? I…need him to bring me something."

Darcy leaned aside to scan the area for any nearby hospital personnel, then lowered her voice. "Yes. I believe I have what you need. Do you trust me, Professor?" She withdrew the medikit from her coat pocket. "I'm told I'd make a good nurse."

Sibelius looked at her with a twinkle in his gray eyes. "I trust you implicitly, my dear." He obediently rolled up his sleeve.

Darcy smiled and prepared the syringe with their new serum. In a few seconds, she'd delivered the injection and hid the kit away again. "I think you'll see the benefits immediately," she said.

The professor leaned back against his stack of pillows,

content to let the medicine take effect. "Damn good thing," he said. "Get out of this stuffy joint. Had the weirdest dream last night. Hospitals, hmph," he snorted. "Damn worst place to get any decent sleep."

"What did you dream about?" she prodded.

"That someone tried to kill me. I thought I'd woken up, then suddenly this strange man, a kid really, stood over me and tried to asphyxiate me. I really thought I'd died...he said "Goodnight Professor," and the next thing I knew, I woke up with this magazine in my hands."

As he held it up, Darcy recognized it as a copy of Maxim.

They both giggled. "Well, maybe you'll have some really nice dreams, now," she said, gesturing to the soft-porn mag.

*

When she returned to McCaine's Pharmacy, she found most of the visitors had departed. Valor was already up from his nap, working in the lab again. In all the commotion, she'd almost forgotten about Oliviah. The cat hadn't been seen since she'd been taken prisoner two days ago. She wandered over to Shania's room, to see if there'd been any improvement.

Audra now sat guard over her, monitoring her temperature and mopping her face with a cold cloth.

"Hi, mom."

Audra turned toward her and smiled. "Hi. I'm so glad you're safe. I shudder to think what might have happened if your message hadn't gotten through to me, or I hadn't the strength to come to you. It's been so long since we've been able to talk that way."

"I know. Did you get your shot? I think the serum should unblock those pathways. What about Grandma? We should get her inoculated as soon as possible too."

"Yes. I'll take some of the serum with me," Audra said.

Darcy nodded toward Shania. "How's she doing?"

Audra bobbed her head side to side. "Holding her own. Dr. McCaine suspects that because she'd been exposed to the virus for such a prolonged period, it may take longer for the serum to reverse the damage. Time. That's all she needs." She nodded toward the hallway. "I think that young warlock has an interest in her. That's good medicine, too," she said with a wink.

"You mean FarRell?" Darcy blushed. "Yes. You'd be surprised what a little bit of…love…can get you through," she said.

Audra stood and gave her daughter a hug. "What about you? How did you meet Dr. McCaine? He's awfully handsome. You could use a little romance yourself."

"Val and I, that is, Dr. McCaine and I, have a working relationship, Mom. I can't say for sure where it may go from here. But you're right. He is awfully handsome."

"I have to leave soon. I'm flying home in a few hours," Audra said. "The regular way," she added. "I think you'll be very busy handing out serum for the next several weeks."

Darcy nodded. "Maybe FarRell and his group will help distribute it. We can't possibly administer everyone ourselves. Before you go," she paused.

"Yes, dear?"

"I've lost Oliviah. She was sick, I found her on my be., I thought she was dying. I brought her here, and that's when all hell broke loose. Shania and I were kidnapped, and since I've been back there's no trace of her. I feel like I've killed her. I'm so sorry. You and Grandma both had her. I'm not fit to be her keeper."

Audra took a long breath in. "Darcy, these things happen. Oliviah is special. She's lived a long time. If she really is gone, be happy for her. She's seen more of life than anyone or anything. But she has a habit of turning up when you least expect her. Don't fear for the worst just yet. Maybe she'll come back as…I don't know. Elizabeth Taylor."

Darcy shook her head. "Elizabeth who? What are you talking about?"

Audra laughed and reached for her coat. "Never mind. When they say cats have nine lives, they don't mean they live the same life nine times. They borrow it from someone else."

"You mean like, reincarnation?"

Audra nodded. "The only difference being, they get to keep all the memories of their previous lives, add them to the pile of knowledge. Can you imagine having that much knowledge? Or that much regret, pain, happiness, friendship? I suppose it's both a blessing and a burden." She donned her coat and gave Darcy one last hug. "Anyway, I've got to get back to Phoenix and your Grandma. Take care of yourself, and get to know that nice doctor a bit better. See you soon."

She saw her mother to the door, and waved goodbye. The mysteriously opportune taxi waited outside. Valor really must have some kind of pipeline to the taxi companies around here. She returned to the lab to seek him out. He stood alone re-organizing things and labeling equipment.

"Hi," she said, leaning her elbows on the lab counter. "Did you have a nice rest?"

Valor's gorgeous violet eyes burned bright once more. "Best ever. A shame your sleep-aid can't be bottled and sold over the counter. Really works well."

Darcy pulled a pouty smile. "Well, it can be bought. Just ask any hooker. But I'm glad you liked my brand. Where is everyone?"

"Gone to spread the word, I imagine. We're going to have

a commercial lab mass-produce the *Sanguis Prima*. Couldn't possibly do it from here."

"Sanguis Prima?"

Valor nodded, then snapped his fingers. "Oh, right. I didn't get a chance to tell you. The serum was the Professor's formula. I found it in his files the night he asked me to go to his office. That's where I got all the chemicals. Including the Thiopental, incidentally.

"*Sanguis Prima*," she repeated. "It means First Blood."

"Uh-huh. I think you know whose blood we are talking about."

Darcy nodded and bowed her head. "My father." She changed the subject. "Val. Did you see Oliviah? I left her here the night we were taken. She was sick, I found her on my bed when I went home from the conference. I thought you could help her."

Valor put the last of his stores and equipment away and came around to Darcy's side of the counter. He put his arm around her. "Yes, she was here," he said, his voice solemn.

"Well, what happened? Why didn't you tell me before?"

"There wasn't time, Darcy. I'm sorry. I did all I could."

Darcy looked panic-stricken. "What do you mean? What did you do with her?"

"Shhh," he soothed. "I tried. I think she contracted the Némesati, too. I didn't know animals could get it. I gave her the herbal serum you and I made the night before. It was all we had."

"What did you do with her," she repeated, her voice rising in near hysteria. She pushed away from Valor's embrace.

"She's still here," he said. He went to retrieve the bundle from the meat locker and saw the ball of cotton sheets inside the mesh basket. But that was all. Oliviah had disappeared. He pulled the wads of sheeting out and looked at Darcy, perplexed. "I wrapped her in these, and put her in the chiller unit. Until we could bury her. But she's gone."

Darcy began to cry. "How could you? How could you? You didn't know if the serum would work on a live subject!"

"She was dying, Darcy. She told me herself, and she didn't fear death. She said they were old acquaintances."

Darcy turned her back on him and ran into the outer room, sobbing. Valor stuffed the sheets in the trash bin and went after her. "Darcy. She'd lived a full life. Fuller than you know."

She rounded on him. "How would you know? You only just met her."

"We talked. A lot. In a language that's been dead for centuries. Have you any idea of that animal's age? She made me look like a toddler by comparison."

Just then, a scratching noise at the window caught their attention. Like metal against glass, the hideous sound raised the hair on their necks and made them shiver. Darcy moved to the window, reached out her hand to part the curtains. There, on the windowsill outside, sat Oliviah, one paw pressed to the glass, claws out. Her golden eyes peered in at her, but they were not the same. Their hue had darkened to a denser, richer shade, like amber.

"Oh, you! You crazy, senseless thing! Where have you been?" Darcy bawled, opening the window and scooping the animal from her perch.

"Outside, in the night, like always. It's the only time you fools let me out."

She squeezed the feline tight in her arms. "Don't you ever do this again, you wretched cat. Don't you ever leave me."

"Leave you? You're stuck with me. Nine lives, Goldilocks, and I've got a few left in me. Can't get rid of the family curse that easily."

With that, she squirmed free of Darcy's embrace and

leapt to the floor, bolting full tilt toward Valor. He crouched down with his hands on his knees, preparing for her playful attack. Instead, she skidded to a stop and rubbed against him in typical cat fashion, performing a figure eight between his legs. Then she sat back on her haunches, staring him down.

"What?" he asked her, aloud this time.

"Do you not recognize me, my love?"

Valor stared into the glowing, fiery amber of her eyes, and his heart twisted. *"Artizia…"*

He lifted the furry body in his arms, his composure starting to crack. *"Artizia…how can this be? Why would you return to me like this? How can I love you as a beast instead of a woman? This will be too difficult, having you around."*

"Hey," Darcy said, interrupting his wordless conversation with Oliviah. "What's this? The clinical-hearted doctor has a soft spot after all? Give me back my cat."

Valor looked up, lovingly stroking Oliviah's spotted coat. "Of course," he said, swallowing hard. He handed the animal to Darcy.

Oliviah settled herself into the crook of Darcy's arm and regarded Valor from a distance. *"I won't stand in your way. Your heart belongs to another now. A human, a mortal. Well, semi-mortal,"* she corrected. *"You have done a great thing. You've saved all of witchkind, for generations to come. Be proud of that. I know I am."*

Chapter Twenty Two

Newborn rays of light beamed through a crack in the curtains and across the rumpled bed. Valor awoke and rolled over onto his side, away from the window. He opened his eyes and took in the lovely curves of a beautiful woman lying next to him. Most of the bedcovers had slipped off during the night. Her delicate spine made an s-curve down the centre of her naked back.

Red-gold curls cascaded over her shoulders and onto the pillow on which she lay her head. Valor reached out to trace his index finger along the ridges of her beautifully carved shoulder blades, then down one arm. He pushed the remaining sheets away, uncovering the sexy curve of her hip and round, juicy ass cheeks. He loved those round cheeks, from the very first day he'd met her in his pharmacy.

That had been a year ago. Now she lay here, his wife, his bright strawberry light, in his bed and in his life, for however long the future had in mind for them. He let his hand glide around the contours of her buttocks, pausing to let his finger explore just a little bit in the space between her cheeks.

Her lungs filled with air as she awoke to his touch. She

rolled toward him, so that her shoulders rested against his chest. Her legs nudged apart, inviting him to explore further. While he had every intention of doing so, he could not resist the pale orbs of her breasts that now revealed themselves.

He cupped them in one hand, squeezing their youthful firmness and thumbing the little brown berries of her nipples. They peaked hard in the still air. She sighed in contentment, and his cock grew hard in anticipation. He reached between her thighs that she had obligingly spread apart, and found the needy nub of flesh that would send her into orgasm. Her pussy already moist, he stroked her clit in easy, slow passes, bringing her closer and closer to climax. Her breathing escalated, and she let out soft little moans.

"That's it, baby, let me take you there," he whispered. He picked up the pace, pumping her pussy harder and faster.

"Oh, Val…" she said. "Yes, sweetheart, that feels good… don't stop. Make me come."

"I'll make you come, baby," he replied. His own cock throbbed and ached as her ass cheeks rubbed against him. He wanted to be in her, soon. But he enjoyed giving her pleasure every bit as much as his own satisfaction, so he kept on, reveling in her tiny squeals of ecstasy along the way.

When he knew she was close, he paused and rolled her onto her back. Her golden hair fell across her face, and she threw her arms over her head, her taut breasts in full view. He virtually swallowed them, taking all of them he could into his mouth and sucking hard.

Her voice turned to little grunts with each breath in and out, her tits heaving as she arched her back beneath him. His teeth grazed each nipple and she cried out in pleasure. He traced a path of kisses down her belly and nuzzled the auburn curls of hair that covered her mound. He liked a hairy pussy.

He ran his palms under her thighs and pushed her legs

into a bent position, rendering her pretty pussy unobstructed. Her swollen clit bulged out from between her labia, red and wet and wanting. His tongue was all over it, licking, sucking, teasing it back and forth and dipping into the cleft on either side.

She was virtually screaming now, calling out for release. "Val," she cried. "Oh, Val, please, baby…"

He pressed the whole of his tongue flat against her cunt and licked it upwards, then downwards, repeating this motion until she tumbled over the edge into orgasm. Her whole body shook, her hips bucked up and down, her hands clutched the headboard and her head thrashed from side to side. He kept his tongue working at her until her tremors ceased.

Her pussy dripped with his saliva. He drew back and placed his hands on her hips, easing her over onto her belly. He would take his pleasure now, any way he wanted. She was very accommodating, his new little wife. He patted her round buns and placed one knee on either side of her. He eased her hips up off the surface of the bed. He liked her with her ass in the air.

His cock slid easily into her wet space, and he pushed to the hilt. Being so young, her parts were tight as gun barrels and he liked that too; the sensation of his erect cock filling her completely as he stroked in and out.

"There's my sweet little scientist," he said, breathing hard. "Always ready for an experiment." He drove into her several more times, until fully coated in her cream and her wetness. Then he withdrew, and rubbed the swollen head of his cock in the little rosebud of her ass. He could hear her breath coming in pants, her hands fisting and re-fisting the pillows under her head.

"Just relax, baby," he whispered. He sucked his thumb and pressed it to her ass, priming the opening even further. He rubbed her back, easing her tension, and at the right moment, slid his cock into her rectum. She made a squawking noise, muffled by the pillow, but did not resist. He could feel the muscles of her sphincter yielding, and the head of his cock passing through it nice and slow.

Then he was all the way in, her ass tighter even than her pussy, and this aroused him immensely. He kept the rhythm slow and even, relishing every inch of her canal, taking care not to cause her pain as he drove toward his goal, his release.

Another stroke, and another…almost there. He climaxed with a last forceful push into her tight little ass, letting everything go, and came harder than he could ever remember in his two centuries of manhood.

His heart raced and his lungs pumped, slowly regaining control as the last of his fluid spilled into her body. He pulled out of her tight little bum, and playfully spanked one cheek.

"Ouch," she barked.

"Ouch? Now you say ouch?" He stretched out overtop her, reaching up to intertwine his hands with hers as they spread-eagled together on the mattress and settled his nose in her hair as she lay face-down.

"Yeah," she said, starting to giggle.

"Nothing else was ouch? Just my spanking?"

"No. The rest was…amazing. Mind-blowing. You are one dynamic doctor," she said, exhaling in contentment.

"Always listen to your doctor," he added.

"Always," she agreed.

"Always."

Valor's head snapped up, looking around the room, but not in time to see the vexatious furball land on his back with all fours. "Aaagh," he yelled, as the nubs of Oliviah's claws dug into his skin.

"Oh don't be such a wuss, I didn't even have my claws out," she chided him.

"Were you spying on us? Did you enjoy yourself?" he asked in their private language.

"No, I was not. But I enjoyed making you scream just now."

Valor bucked the animal off him, and she jumped to the pillow next to Darcy's head.

"And how are you this morning, Goldilocks? Having fun with Doctor Dreamy?" Oliviah asked, switching to English.

"Go away," Darcy said aloud. "Can't we have a little privacy, please? Do you have to share in everything, you little pest?"

Oliviah pawed the pillow in a circle, settling herself down in the resulting indentation. *"Maybe not everything. But you're stuck with me. Nine lives, Sunshine."*

"Right. All of them borrowed. Who's life did you swipe this time, Elizabeth Taylor's?" Darcy asked with sarcasm.

The cat looked at her with eyes that resembled great amber moons. *"Elizabeth who?"*

"Elizabeth who?" Valor echoed, rolling over to lay beside Darcy on the bed.

Darcy laughed. "Come now, Val. Certainly you must be old enough to know who that is."

"I don't, actually. What are you talking about?"

"Don't you know why cats have nine lives? They steal them from dead people," Darcy said, punctuating her statement by sticking her tongue out at Oliviah.

"Oh." Valor said, his voice subdued. "I do now." He shook his head. "But I still don't know who Elizabeth Taylor is."

"Me neither, until I looked her up on Google. She was an actress, very famous. Considered to be one of the most beautiful women in the world. She had dark, blue-black hair, and violet eyes, something like yours," Darcy continued.

"But could be a real witch to work with, sometimes." She caught herself, and added, "No pun intended."

Valor's face sported a lopsided smile. "None taken. Violet, huh? Well that proves it, then. She's not Elizabeth Taylor."

"No?"

"No," Valor said firmly. "She's just one of the family now. My family."

With that, Oliviah trained her very non-Taylor-esque eyes on him.

"Well, how can I argue with that. Always listen to your doctor," Oliviah said, in a voice for both to hear.

Darcy smiled and turned to look at her husband. "Always."

The End

From the Author

Thank you for reading this book. I sincerely hope you enjoyed it, and if so, the favor of a customer review would be appreciated.

Please visit:
www.amazon.com/The-Witch-Doctor
and let me know what you thought.

*

Visit my official online hangouts:
idreamofjean.com
thejeanjournal.com
facebook.com/authorjeanmaxwell
@dearjeanmaxwell

*

For exclusive content and up-to-the-minute details on New Releases and Works-In-Progress, please join my mailing list by sending an email to:
dearjeanmaxwell@gmail.com
subject: **mailing list**

*

Yours in words,
Jean Maxwell

Made in the USA
Charleston, SC
12 July 2014